Some of this is Real

Short Stories
by Jack Billings

Copyright 2020

Spencer Hollow Publishing

PO Box 51149
Eugene, OR 97405
First Edition

ISBN: 9798616469601

With the exception of brief quotes used in reviews or scholarly articles, no part of this book may be transmitted, forwarded, stored, copied, downloaded or reproduced in any manner without the express permission of the author, agent, publisher, or legally recognized copyright holder.

Dedications

For my loving wife, Linda, whose encouragement and editing skills have made this collection possible.

And, to good friend and mentor, Mike Bonner, whose publishing talents brought the stories to print.

Finally, for the Vero Café writing group whose inspiration and humor kept me going.

Cover Image by Don Dubin Photography

Some of this is Real

Short Stories by Jack Billings

Table of Contents

Dedications/Page 4

Table of Contents/Page 5

The So What/Page 7

The Waiting Rooms/Page 27

The Orion/Page 41

Old Spot/Page 63

The Phone Call/Page 67

An Agnostic's Journey/Page 89

The Interrogation/Page 107

Acknowledgments Notes on the Stories/Page 133

About the Author/Page 136

The So What

The So What Tavern squatted on the corner of East 4th and Vine, just up the street from the old Illinois Central roundhouse. Torn awnings and peeling paint were some of the more obvious of its chronic, cosmetic problems. Unseen were the termite infested floor joists that gave way when Virden Creek flooded and sent raw sewage down the pitted asphalt.

Eddie Wandro did as little as possible to put the So What back in business after the health department unreasonably used the sanitation problem as an excuse to close him down. With patched plumbing and a shored-up foundation, Eddie reopened a few days later, and the regulars were back the same afternoon. Ever economical with the truth, he told the authorities just enough to keep them at bay until the next inundation.

Eddie was short and fat, bald and perpetually red-faced. He celebrated his Czech heritage as proud people always under threat from their German neighbors. His paternal grandfather immigrated in 1890 to avoid conscription. The family name was homogenized at Ellis Island; the strong Catholic faith endured.

He bought the tavern in 1948, when it was known as the Roundhouse. He re-named it the So What in 1959 in honor of the jazz tune by Miles Davis. The only music in the place came from the Wurlitzer juke box, which made up in volume what it lacked in variety. Though he needed it only twice, Eddie kept a 24-inch baseball bat under the bar.

De facto housing segregation ruled cities like Waterloo, Iowa. By deep-seated bias and custom, people of color could only live on the East Side and then between the rail yard and Conger Avenue. Many deeds prohibited ownership by minorities. Banks red-lined loan applications. Negroes could not find a home for sale or an apartment to rent on the other side of the Cedar River. Social norms hemmed them in as effectively as *de jure* segregation in Montgomery, Alabama. Their part of town, originally called Smokey Row, now the North End, was just up Fourth behind the rail yard.

Large numbers of Negroes could trace their Waterloo origins to Holmes County, Mississippi, and the Illinois Central railroad strike of 1911. As strike breakers they eventually represented more than 10% of the East Side's populace. Crossing picket lines added economic animus to pervasive racial hatred. By 1959, their numbers had grown, and they increasingly competed with whites for housing and jobs outside the North End. Eddie's customers were all Caucasian variants, and some began to move away. Revenue slumped and Eddie fretted more each week.

****

The other businesses on the block with the So What were: Lottie's Hair Design, Tweed Treasures Used Clothing and the Mosby Funeral Home. Eddie got on well enough with the owners, especially Lottie Collins. Although keeping the custom of serving whites only, he was known to share a stein with her some afternoons in the back. Several times she brought her husband, Curtis.

One afternoon, Lottie and Curtis offered a novel suggestion: convert the storeroom off Vine to an adjacent bar for Negroes. In 1955, "Separate but equal" schools had failed legally in the United States Supreme Court. But the concept of white only bars was alive and well in Waterloo until well after the Fair Accommodations Act of 1964.

A divided tavern could use a common cooler, deliveries and inventory, although it would need a separate manager and employees, entrance, bathrooms, pool tables and sound system. A pass through hallway with a door at each end provided access. An old casement window stashed in the back was installed to provide some light.

No one who knew Eddie believed the adjacent arrangement was a product of his social progress. Eddie was as racist as the next white person, but minority dollars paid the bills as well as any. Since he knew no Negroes beyond his neighbors, he needed Lottie's help with hiring a manager. She brought him Willie Hoosman. He was smooth faced, flashed a big smile, knew everyone and proved tough enough to handle problems needing less than police involvement.

Willie understood well the opportunity laid before him as manager of the new venue. Eddie needed someone to trust. The manager tracked the money, paid the help, ordered inventory and kept the peace. Though he was big enough to handle most problems, he maintained a switchblade in his back pocket.

He harbored plans to open his own tavern someday on the far side of the North End, on the way to Evansdale. He dreamed of a small stage available for Saturday night local talent, with a BBQ smoker in the back.

Once the remodeling was complete, Eddie opened the Side Pocket on Vine Street without fanfare. Word spread, and soon he saw an uptick in his revenues. There was some grumbling about the "coloreds" on the other side of the wall, yet Eddie's customers understood his economic plight.

Though sharing a building, the So What and the Side Pocket had little in common. Those who entered the respective establishments were neighbors only in general. Many from both sides of the dividing wall were graduates of East High, but they did not know one another.

Eddie's patrons were all white and nearly all male. Many worked at the Rath Packing slaughterhouse over by the river. A currently hot topic on the bar stools was Black Hawk County's order that the meat packer cease dumping offal into the Cedar.

On occasion off-duty police officers would take the back booth. They kept to themselves; their presence had a calming effect on the other patrons. One of them, Bob Murphy, lived on the East Side, beyond Donald Street, and occasionally came in by himself. "Murph" as everyone called him, had served as a marine platoon sergeant in the Pacific. He was sworn in six years ago and was on the rise in the department. Maintaining a working relationship with leaders in the North End was vital to his vision of policing.

The Waterloo Police Department reflected the demographics of white control over the city. Although Negroes represented about 15% of the East Side population, the department swore in its first black officer, James Brown, in 1953. He did not last long. The second was James W. Cook, in 1967, who eventually retired from the department. Generally, the officers did not go into the North End unless blood was spilled. Their interactions with minorities usually occurred on the margin and almost always ended poorly.

Eddie's regulars included Tom Sullivan. He and his wife, Alleta, lost their five sons all at once when the USS Juneau was torpedoed in 1942. For a time, Tom and Alleta toured the country selling war bonds. The celebrity status soon wore off, but the agony endured. He usually sat on the far left and always by himself. Grief was permanently etched in his face.

Besides the county's effort to clean up the river, usual topics were sports and politics. On a typical afternoon, Tom's longtime friend, Ozzie Svoboda, sat a few stools to the right. He flicked the end of his cigarette in the direction of the ashtray and exhaled more acrid blue smoke into the overhead haze. Hunched over the bar, he grabbed more peanuts from the greasy bowl in front of him. Like Eddie, he was proud of his Czech heritage and was a staunch Roman Catholic.

Moving about on the stool, and clearing his throat, Ozzie signaled the start of one of his pronouncements. "Mark my words," he growled in his smoker's voice to no one in particular, "that Kennedy guy from back East is gonna run for president."

Unmoved, Eddie placidly dried glasses behind the bar. Tom Sullivan looked over and asked, "You think a Catholic will ever be elected president?"

"Maybe if he has a Baptist running mate."

"He'd have to beat Nixon."

With that exchange, politics trailed off for the moment and both men went back to their beers.

****

Like all her family and most of her friends, Eddie's neighbor down the block, Lottie Collins, was officially a member of the Mount Calvary Missionary Baptist Church on Jackson Street. She and Curtis usually attended Sunday morning service, but seldom came on Wednesday night. She suffered Waterloo's racial segregation and bias as a norm to be outmaneuvered, not accepted.

Lottie grew up on Cottage Street and like most of the children in the North End, she attended Hayes Elementary School. There were no white students at Hayes. Lottie first met white classmates when she entered Logan Junior High School, but both races kept to themselves.

At 14, she began hair styling for her sisters and friends, using the Madam C.J. Walker method. Her beauty parlor launched in 1950 and specialized in wigs and the harsh products then available for nappy hair. Every Negro woman remembered the day her hair was first straightened with a combination of chemicals or a heated metal comb. Natural styles like the Afro were years in the future.

Most of her customers were middle-aged and expected to spend several hours in her chair. They talked about their men and kids, gossiped about the neighbors, commented on the church pastor and held forth generally on life.

****

Dante "Tiny" Ellis grew up on the South Side of Chicago and had received valuable education and life skills training from detention centers and a short stint in prison. He was a very large man apparently born with no neck; his head sat directly on his shoulders. A deep crease marked his forehead in contrast to an ever-present thin smile. His prominent snake-like eyes seemingly never blinked as they slowly scanned the doorway and sidewalk outside. Anyone who came into his view became an object of interest, perhaps as something to eat. You could outrun Tiny, but you wouldn't want him to get hold of you.

No one, including Willie, knew why Tiny came west to Iowa. It was rumored that he had jumped parole in Chicago because of a warrant for his arrest, but he never spoke of it himself.

When he first entered the Side Pocket, Tiny marked Willie as the manager and offered to buy him a drink. Because he was officially on duty, and had not seen Ellis before, he politely declined. You never knew who the Liquor Commission might send in under cover.

Preliminary niceties out of the way, Tiny ordered his own beer and a shot. He was accompanied by a rough looking character introduced as Sledge. There was a four-top table in the back corner near the casement window. Two young regulars, Willie's friends, were deep in conversation. They looked up uneasily when Tiny and Sledge strolled over to the table. "Y'all don't mind if we sit here, do you?"

Although the words were neutral, Tiny's deep voice carried a distinct menace. The young men apparently remembered an important engagement and quickly excused themselves. Thus, began Tiny's near permanent presence every afternoon in the back corner. Most knew Tiny had money to lend, no questions asked. The amounts were usually small, the terms short and the interest high. There was no need for a reserved sign; everyone shortly understood that this was his table and he was open for business.

Occasionally one of Tiny's borrowers would come up short. Interest was applied at 10% per day. Two days delinquent would bring a knock at the door or an ugly confrontation with Sledge.

Overt violence was not Tiny Ellis' preferred method for collection of overdue accounts. Threats of broken arms or dislocated shoulders usually went far enough without the messiness of hospital treatment. Usury and extortion among the minority denizens of the North End was of no interest to the all-white Police Department. Blacks' enmity toward police meant no intimidation was reported. So, if Tiny, or more likely Sledge, avoided permanent damage in emptying pockets, law enforcement was not a concern.

Tiny's presence at the tavern made Willie edgy. The big man was careful to avoid drama at his table and all his transactions took place somewhere else. Willie also figured that Tiny had other sources of income since the loan business seemed too small scale for the cash he flashed. Still, Willie could see the potential for problems that would threaten his status. He heard that a local regular, Leroy Redd, owed Ellis money but likely didn't have it.

As they counted inventory, Willie decided to tell Eddie about Tiny's back corner operation.

"You think he's hurtin' business?" Eddie mused, totaling the number of kegs. "Maybe some of your people are stayin' away because of him?"

"I don't know, Mr. Wandro," Willie replied. "He ain't caused no trouble, but I heard his man Sledge has been looking for one of our regulars. He's got a local kid, Jerome Jenkins, with him.

"So, what do you want to do?" Eddie asked. He wanted things quiet on Willie's side of the wall.

****

Janette Redd, like many of Lottie Collins' clientele, had come to her for years; she began styling Janette's hair when they attended junior high. The librarian at East High, Janette had a standing appointment for Friday afternoon at 3 pm. She now occupied Lottie's chair and was clearly distressed.

Never shy about her intuition, Lottie draped the cloth around her longtime friend and asked, "What's up, girl, you bothered by somethin." As she looked at Janette in the opposite wall's mirror, she realized that her eyes were red; she had been crying.

"It's Leroy," she sighed. "Two guys came to my office this afternoon. I was by myself because school was out. They said they were looking for him because he owes money to that shark, Tiny. I think one of them was Juanita Jenkins' boy, but I didn't recognize the other. He looked real mean. He sounded like he was from Chicago. They didn't like me saying I didn't know where Leroy was at. They said they would "drop by" tonight and expected him to be home."

"Tiny? You mean the big guy down at the Side Pocket, back in the corner by the window? Why would Leroy borrow money from him? He's dangerous."

"That's what I heard, too. Leroy's been tryin' to impress a girl in a tight dress. Those guys said he owes Tiny $100 and is two days late. He adds $10 a day interest."

"Damn, girl" was all Lottie could say.

****

Leroy Redd had inherited his mother's height and slender build, but none of her ambition and little of her intelligence. Because he could not hold a job, he still lived at home and cadged money from Janette every week. He was always chasing after the "next great thing" which inevitably took what he had and left him with nothing.

Unfortunately, his financial needs had taken a steep climb after he met Wilma Rawlings at the Side Pocket. She could defy gravity by squeezing her substantial curves into a skinny dress, exposing 40% of her bosom and leaving no doubt about the heft of the rest. Leroy was not alone in seeking her attention, but he wasn't able to apply much juice to his approach.

Tiny's loan business was not the only enterprise operating out of the Side Pocket. Wilma usually sat alone at the bar for a while, until some man joined her and bought a round. After a drink and some small talk, they would leave together. About an hour later, Wilma would come back alone, and resume her place at the bar. Leroy was slow on the uptake, but he eventually caught the drift. He hitched up his nerve and inquired about the cost of the honey pot.

The next afternoon, when his "allowance" from his mother had run out, he sidled over to Tiny's table. Both Ellis and Sledge gave him a wary look.

"Hey, Mr. Tiny, how y'all doin?"

"Who are you? "growled Sledge, boring into Leroy's soul with slits for eyes. "You invited over here?"

"Go easy, Herman, the boy just came over to say 'hello'. Right, son?" Tiny looked Leroy up and down with his serpentine eyes. "Have a seat, I'll buy you a beer. You drinkin' Hamm's? What's your name?"

After the beers had arrived, Tiny peered at Leroy, "So, what you want, young fella?"

Thus began a series of loans that stretched over several weeks. At first, Leroy was able to repay on time, including interest. But Tiny was a patient man. He had correctly sized up that Redd's appetite for seeking Wilma's intermittent attention would outstrip his ability to keep his financial commitments.

The Wednesday his last loan came due, Leroy sat at the bar, nursing a beer purchased with his few remaining dollars. Trying to pay Tiny with $25 dollars, when $100 was owed, was worse than offering nothing. His mother refused to give him more cash. He decided to leave before Tiny came in, but he had no idea what to do.

In addition to Sledge, Tiny was usually accompanied by Jerome Jenkins, who grew up over on Newell Street. For the last few weeks Jerome had been absent, though no one at the Side Pocket then knew why. After a while he returned and resumed his place behind Tiny in the corner. It later became known that Jerome's absence was the product of a jail term down in Des Moines.

****

Sledge's threat to come by Janette's place that night prompted Lottie to wake Curtis at home. He quickly agreed she should not be alone, and he arrived at her place about 6 pm. He could stay until it was time for him to leave for work. He had hit the grand slam home run: a night shift, AFL/CIO benefits job at the John Deere foundry across the river. Though quiet by nature, Curtis was a big man who understood the value of size in certain circumstances. This was one of those times.

Curtis and Janette both jumped from a rough knock on the front door about 7 pm. Curtis opened the door a crack and faced Sledge and Jerome.

"Where's Leroy?", Sledge snapped, surprised to see a large man at the door. "Send him out here. He done forgot he owes Mr. Ellis money and he's late."

"He's not here" Curtis replied calmly. "We don't know where he is. I don't think he's coming back here, not now anyways."

"Well, when you see that little piece of shit, you tell him he already owes $120 and it goes up $10 every day. And, Ellis won't wait any longer."

"Oh, I'll tell him---when I see him."

Frustrated that Leroy was not at home, and because he could not get past the big man to intimidate Janette, Sledge turned toward a lowered Cadillac at the curb. Curtis heard car doors open, but no dome light came on. From the curtain in the living room, he watched the Caddy pull away.

"Janette, I can stay until 11:30, then I have to go to work. Lottie told me to take you over to our place when I leave."

****

From a hiding place across the street, Leroy saw Sledge and Jerome approach his mother's house. He could not hear the conversation on the front porch but divined its meaning.

He waited in the shadows as the Cadillac slowly drove away; eventually, he watched as Curtis and his mother left. He still needed to sleep and change clothes, so Leroy worked his way across the dark street. As he rounded the corner of the house, he suddenly fell hard. For a moment he lost track of time and place. His head felt on fire; he was bleeding above his eyebrow.

Sledge's whiskey tainted breath was in his ear. "Thought you could sneak by us, boy? Forget your promises? Where's Tiny's money?" He still held the leather sap he had applied to Leroy's forehead.

"I—I—I ain't got it, but I will. I got a line on it for Monday."

"What you talkin' about, Monday? You owed the money last Wednesday." Leroy took a swift kick in the ribs and howled in agony.

"Get up, you little piece of shit. Come with us."

They duck-walked him back out to the street, one on each side. The Cadillac was again in the shadows at the curb. Sledge pulled open the back door and shoved him in. Tiny already occupied most of the back seat. Sledge and Jerome took the front.

"Why, Leroy we been lookin' for you; you been avoiding your old friend Tiny."

****

As Leroy cowered in the back seat, Tiny explained the fundamentals of his operation. You could pay him back in cash or in kind. Money was straightforward, but a working payment was more complicated. Sledge could always use some local talent in debt collection, both to back him up, and to identify who owed what.

Jerome Jenkins had seen the light and signed on when his own loan fell delinquent. But other problems caught up with him, and Tiny revealed that he was on his way to another stretch in jail. More help was timely.

Though dumb as a post, Leroy was desperate; he needed a way out. There was no real prospect for cash on Monday and the next collection effort would hurt a lot more. How much "work" would suffice to pay off his loan was open ended, but Leroy didn't think of that; he only wanted out of that car. Stark fear overruled any moral qualms.

****

Lottie brought Janette back home the next morning. Coming into the kitchen, they gasped at Leroy's bruised head and large, self-applied bandage. Under intense grilling from both, he eventually admitted what happened the night before. They could easily see he was in real trouble. Before he just owed money. Now he had agreed to engage in mayhem for a certified gangster. Drastic measures were needed. Going to the police directly was not only dangerous, it could backfire.

****

Eddie had unlocked the front door and pulled the string on the neon Hamm's sign when the phone rang.

"Mr. Wandro, it's Lottie. I need your help."

The use of his surname emphasized the seriousness of her call. She hurriedly outlined Leroy's predicament.

He acknowledged Tiny's operation out of the Side Pocket. "But, Lottie, Willie says he ain't causin' problems over there. You want me to throw him out when he ain't doin' anything the police will back me up on. I don't want to get involved."

Drawing up her emotions, she poured out, "Mr. Wandro, Janette is like my sister. We grew up together. I started stylin' her hair when we were in junior high. I was there when Leroy was born. We really need your help. Willie told me there may be a warrant out for this guy."

There was silence on the other end. Long seconds passed. "Shit." After a couple more seconds, he sighed, "I'll see what I can do."

****

Third watch ended at 7 am and several of the officers now in street clothes came in, including Bob Murphy. While the rest occupied the back booth, Eddie motioned Bob up to the bar and outlined the dilemma.

"You're saying that this kid won't come talk to us, and the shark isn't doing anything wrong in the Side Pocket. But you want us to throw him out for good? My supervisor wouldn't like it, and neither do I."

"You don't have to tell him anything. I got an idea."

About 2 in the afternoon, Officer Murphy, now in uniform, parked his patrol car across Vine from the Side Pocket, and got out. He looked at the back corner, through the casement window. With a glance up and down the block, he strode across and went in. Like the So What on the other side of the wall, there was a blue haze, barely illuminated by the dim lights. By prearrangement, Willie was behind the bar. At the doorway, the officer scanned the room. A very large man occupied the table in the back, accompanied by several others. The room went silent. Even the pool players stood up and watched.

Bob Murphy began to doubt his sanity. He had just entered a Negro tavern alone, wearing his uniform, when he was officially off-duty. He had not been called there for service. He was doing a favor for a black woman and her boy, who he didn't know.

Willie had Eddie's baseball bat under the bar and his switchblade in his pocket. If there was an indication of trouble, he was to pull on his ear. The men in the back were motionless, as though frozen.

Murphy pulled a piece of paper from his shirt pocket. "Hey, Willie, I'm looking for someone from Chicago and we heard he might be over here. His name's Ellis, Dante Ellis." From years of practice, he spoke loudly enough to be heard, even in the back, but was not shouting.

"Ellis?", Willie replied, also projecting his voice. "No, Officer Murphy, I don't recognize that name. What's he look like?"

"Well, I understand he is a big man, but we won't have a mug shot for a few more days. I'll bring it by here when I get it. He's wanted in Chicago for assault."

"If I hear anything, I'll tell Mr. Wandro."

Stuffing the paper back in his uniform, Officer Murphy moved toward the door. He looked pointedly at the back corner on his way out. Immediately after the patrol car pulled from the curb, Tiny, Sledge and Jerome got up to leave.

"You done good, Willie," Ellis said as he settled his tab. "That cop comes back with a picture you still don't know me. Understood?"

Later that afternoon, Eddie called Lottie and related the scene. They agreed that Tiny probably wouldn't risk coming back to the Side Pocket. He heard stifled sounds of relief as Lottie breathed her thanks.

****

The United States Supreme Court's decision in 1955, to end state-ordered school segregation, also signaled the eventual end to other forms of racial exclusion. Although the Fair Accommodations Act was not adopted until 1964, Eddie could see the writing on the wall. He faced integrating his business or shutting down. His regulars would not likely sit next to Negroes at the bar. He didn't want to manage a mostly minority operation himself. And, truth be known, he was getting tired of the daily grind of running a tavern. Although he had brought the bar back from its death bed in 1948, he was no longer a younger man.

Curtis Collins and Willie Hoosman made an odd couple, but both had business sense. Curtis and Lottie had saved a little money they were willing to invest; Willie wanted his own place. So, one afternoon in the back room they proposed to purchase the tavern, with the understanding the wall would come down. The So What as Eddie knew it would be gone for good. He agreed to give them six months to pay him, while they made the transition. They dropped the So What name in favor of the Side Pocket.

Ozzie Svoboda, Tom Sullivan and the other regulars never returned. Neither did Eddie, except driving by occasionally to ascertain the Hamm's sign was still illuminated. The police officers found a different after-hours venue.

Tiny Ellis, Sledge and Wilma Rawlings were also gone for good. Ever the vigilant manager, Willie ran off several problem patrons before they became established. He kept Eddie's baseball bat under the bar and his switchblade in his back pocket. The Hamm's sign in the front window still shown onto Fourth Street. The blue haze now hung uninterrupted from Fourth to Vine. All the customers knew one another. Business flourished.

Then, in January, about a year after the sale, a drunk thrown out of his rooming house crawled under the Side Pocket trying to stay dry and get warm. The heating fire he torched from discarded cardboard and joist repair debris soon engulfed him and the tavern. Lottie's place was spared, but Tweed Treasures lost its inventory to smoke damage. The caskets at Mosby's were unscathed.

The insurance paid the vendor bills, the property taxes and not much else. There was not enough to rebuild. Lottie and Curtis split the remainder with Willie. They were able to expand the hair salon to three chairs. Willie never opened his dream club out toward Evansdale. But, with his winning smile and life-honed people skills, he launched a highly successful insurance business, catering exclusively to the minority community. A convenience store sprang from the ashes at Fourth and Vine. Eddie Wandro moved to Tucson and died within a year. He never returned to Waterloo.

The Waiting Rooms

Chipped, lime green concrete block walls reflected low maintenance. Three rows of unpadded chairs faced the reception. The few windows were placed so high only a few bare branches could be seen. Tiny motes drifted in pale light cast from above. A vaguely antiseptic odor hung in the air. Abrupt blasts of hot air from an overhead vent subsided as the fan exhaled its final energy with a few tepid coughs.

Slumped in one of those chairs was a man, no longer young. Deep arroyos creased his sunken, mahogany cheeks. Long, limp hair, once jet black, was streaked with pewter. Rheumy, dark brown eyes vaguely focused on some carpet pattern a few feet in front of him. A walker was poised nearby. Shifting in his seat as if seeking less pain, he remained silent. The pocket of his snagged flannel shirt held a rumpled pack of cigarettes. His hunched frame belied his once youthful height. The light had all but gone from his eyes.

A younger man lounged next to him, thumbing a well-worn women's magazine. His cowboy style shirt and crisp jeans contrasted strikingly. He glanced at his father with a look that said "no good will come of this" as the clinic intercom periodically chirped requests for assistance or admonished someone to answer line one.

The first hour plodded by despite their timely appearance. Others were called to the desk though they had arrived later. For the third time his son approached the counter, only to be told, again, that it should be only a few minutes more. The old man stifled a ragged cough.

"Hang in there, Dad, we'll go back soon."

At last, a well-nourished woman in scrubs emerged with a chart and called out, "Mr. Caldwell?" Edging forward, the old man reached shaky fingers for his walker and pushed himself to his feet. His son leaned in, hooking his forearm for support. The walker eased ahead, a foot at a time, as both followed the chart woman through swinging double doors. She led them down a hallway and into a small room crowded with examination bed, physician's stool and two molded plastic chairs. Opposite the door was a Formica-clad counter with a stainless-steel sink, several medical instruments, a glass jar filled with tongue depressors and boxes of disposable gloves. The smell of disinfectant was stronger.

"The doctor will see you soon," she said as she closed the door. Again, they waited. The old man slumped down in his chair, winded from the exertion. His son eased against the corner. "Dad, tell me again why we're here."

"Tests," he replied quietly.

"Yeah, you told me, but what kind of tests?" The elder pulled out a ragged handkerchief to catch another watery, congested cough. His answer was interrupted by a soft knock and the entry of a compact, middle-aged man in a white coat with a stethoscope draped around his neck.

Offering his hand, he said "You're Mr. Caldwell? I'm Doctor Phillips. Your regular doctor isn't here today, but we thought you needed these results right away. Is this your son? Is it all right with you that he stays in here with us?"

Sitting on the stool and looking directly into the old man's face, the physician settled himself. He waited until the old man met his gaze.

"Mr. Caldwell, you know that we've been concerned about your cough and how much weight you've lost. That's why we took a biopsy and scans of your chest. It's clear that you have lung cancer and it's serious." The physician paused again. "I've conferred with our radiologist and your left lower lobe is fully involved. We don't know if it has spread, but that's likely."

The old man looked distractedly to the side but said nothing. The son straightened.

"Are there any more tests to run? Should we get a second opinion?"

Phillips replied, "We could refer your dad to another clinic, but that would take time and I'm not sure your insurance would pay for it."

"So, what are his choices?"

Before the physician could answer, the old man coughed hard again and wheezed, "How long?"

****

Except for the scuffing of the walker across the asphalt parking lot, silence draped their journey to the car. The September afternoon sun was fading, and a breeze had picked up. The old man lowered himself heavily into the passenger seat, as his son stored the walker behind him. The acrid smell of cigarette smoke seemed stronger than when they arrived.

They were quickly on Highway 12 toward Leesburg. After some minutes the son asked, "You haven't told Mom, have you?"

A moment passed.

"Dad."

A few beats later, "Dad! You heard what Phillips said, 'six months'! You knew you were sick. I'm your only child and you never told me. And now we have to tell Mom."

Miles passed.

"Why wouldn't you let him tell you about radiation or chemo? That might extend your life, give us more time together."

The old man gaped vacantly out the window. He reached instinctively for a cigarette, then dropped his hand back into his lap.

The son realized he had a death grip on the wheel and was well over the speed limit. He took a deep breath to steady himself and looked over. Even from this morning his father seemed diminished.

The sun shot brilliant yellow-orange rays through the clouds forming over the mountains, but neither man saw them. It would soon be dark, and they were still a half hour away from the old man's home. The wind kicked up again and lofted desiccated weeds across the pavement. The son switched on the headlights and waited while the old man stared at his hands.

"Dad, you have to let me help you. You can't do this alone and mom's not strong enough."

Several minutes passed. "Dammit, Dad, we have to face this together. I'll talk to my foreman; he'll give me some time off. We can take the referral to the hospice."

"I ain't goin' to no dying place."

As they made the turn toward the house, the old man finally forced out, "I'm sorry."

When they reached the driveway, the son pulled the car to the side of his own pick-up. The wife's Honda was parked at the curb behind them. They waited silently for several minutes more. Movement at the curtains confirmed she was inside. Darkness had settled; the porch light came on.

"So, what are you going to tell her? She's been with you 45 years; you have to tell her straight up. She's in there waiting. She was probably thinking you just have pneumonia, but the longer we're out here, the worse she knows it is." Another pause. "What are you going to say?"

"I don't know. I didn't want to worry her." He wheezed into his handkerchief as his gaze drifted toward a distant horizon.

"Dad, remember Edna Blanchard, down the road? You know what she went through. At least you have the VA benefits. We can get some folks in to help and get a hospital bed and set it up in the living room when the time comes." The old man said nothing.

"Dad, we need a plan. You need to decide what to say, then go in and do it."

"Yeah, I will. You go on home; I'll take care of it," the old man sighed.

The son brought the walker to the passenger door and half lifted his father to his feet. As the old man shuffled up the sidewalk toward the front door, the son called behind him,

"Wait, I'm coming in with you."

****

The son opened the creaky screen and pushed in the front door. He held both aside as the old man eased the walker across the threshold. They were greeted by 75-degree heat and cooking smells from the kitchen.

"I'm in here."

The old man pushed his way to the recliner. With a quivering hand he steadied himself before dropping between the over-stuffed arms. He eyed an ashtray filled with tobacco debris, then his gaze slowly drifted around the room. The furniture was all where it had been that morning. Pulling the side lever, he eased back and closed his eyes.

The son moved to the kitchen doorway. Turning from the stove she asked, "Jimmy, can you stay for dinner? I have plenty." She, too, seemed frailer.

"She already knows," he thought. Crossing the tiny kitchen, he wrapped an arm around her thin frame. "I'll check with Susan in a little bit. Right now, Mom, let's turn off the burner. We all need to talk."

With a barely perceptible nod, she wiped her hands and he followed her into the living room. She chose the end of the couch, nearest her husband. His eyes were closed. Jimmy's large hands gently cradled hers. Moments passed.

"Dad, we're here."

Eyes still closed, the old man shifted, seeking more comfort. Finally blinking, he inhaled and coughed at the same time. Looking straight ahead he moistened his lips, shifted again and forced out, "Bernice, I got cancer. It's bad."

The impact of those few words compressed the room. Though her expression remained stoic, she pulled a hanky from her apron pocket and pressed it to her face. Jimmy wrapped his arm around her shoulders and drew her closer. Then her tears came, stifled and forlorn. The old man looked up at the ceiling, then to his wife, "I'm sorry, I didn't know how to tell you. I got six months."

After more tears, she wiped her nose, sighed, and went to her husband. She cradled his face in her hands and met his eyes. "Willis, I'll always be here with you." Kissing him on the head and squeezing his hand, she returned to the kitchen. Over her shoulder she said, "Jimmy, please stay."

"I will, Mom, I'll call Susan."

The old man's eyes closed. Then, he grimaced.

"Dad, you told Dr. Phillips you're in pain."

"All the time."

"For how long now?"

"Awhile."

"So, you got the starter pills he gave us?"

"They're in my jacket pocket."

"I'll get some water for you and I'll go to Lacey's tomorrow. They'll have the full prescription by then. I made sure the doctor told them I would pick it up."

Another pause passed between them. "Son," he said quietly. "I'm scared. Promise me you'll take care of your mother." He coughed three times in succession.

"Dad, you know we will. We'll take care of both of you. We'll work this out together. Don't worry about anything. Whatever needs doing, I can take care of it." Jimmy realized that he was speaking hurriedly, sensing the importance of the moment and his own raw edge.

Willis Caldwell had no capacity for an emotional conversation with his son. Taciturn to an extreme, he grew up without a father. He left home at 16 to escape the trap of his mother's dependence on a succession of "uncles" she used for support and amusement. The only emotion he could express was anger, kept under wraps by iron will. Now, he faced dependence on a son he admired but did not know.

Almost inaudibly Jimmy said, "I'll get the pills". The old man closed his eyes, swallowed hard and leaned back. While the men spoke in the living room, Bernice heard the words "pills" and "pain". She hugged herself and stared beyond the lights next door. *"Oh god, ... cancer...What are we going to do?"*

Bernice turned from the stove as Jimmy reached into the cupboard for a glass. They embraced and she half sobbed some more. "Oh, Jimmy, this is so hard."

****

Later, Jimmy and Susan sat together in their kitchen. She alternately shook her head and nodded as he related the day.

"After Dad left, the doctor told me he might not have even six months. He's in pretty rough shape."

"What did he prescribe?"

Jimmy pulled a slip from his shirt pocket, "It's called dilaudid. I hadn't heard of it before."

"I haven't either. I imagine it's strong stuff. I guess there's no reason to worry about Dad becoming addicted."

"Yeah, I gave him a pill before I left, and he was snoring as I went out the door."

"Did your mom know?"

"She knew something bad was going on. She had found a couple of bloody handkerchiefs buried in the dirty clothes. And, she thought it was strange when he insisted that Freddy Moss take him to the clinic a few weeks ago. They were gone all day. He didn't want anyone to know a biopsy was performed."

"That sounds like him. I'll go over in the morning and make breakfast for them."

"I already called Bob and got the day off. I'll go to Lacey's for the medicine and come over, too. It's probably good to start doing something."

Susan placed her hand on his. "It's horrible, hon, but at least we can help them together. Imagine if your mother had to face this alone."

****

Willis Caldwell had weeks, not months, to live. Once a virile man, his weakened life quickly faded. When the bathroom became too distant, a commode appeared by the recliner. Diapers soon followed. Eventually, his ravaged lungs could not sustain him, and a nebulizer arrived. A hospital bed replaced the recliner when he could no longer get to his feet. Some days, he ate almost nothing.

As his time waned, he slowly opened to his son. There were narrow windows of lucidity between the end of one dose of dilaudid and the pain-driven demand for another.

At first, Willis talked only about his youth after he left home. Revealing more each time, he described his journey across the West in search of work and connection. At 35, he met Bernice and finally discovered affection for someone else. His proposal was a statement, "Reckon we should get married".

Their only child arrived two years later. Willis was proud but had no sense of how to act around his young son. His demanding work schedule kept him from teachers' conferences, school plays, football games, the benchmarks of a child's school life. When he returned home each night, Jimmy was already in bed.

While he was close to his mother, Jimmy did not know his father. Willis was never mean to him, but seldom asked about his dreams, his fears, or his life. Jimmy believed that his father did not care, but only tolerated him. He did not know how to bridge the emotional divide between them.

Now, little remained except emotions. As the disease reduced Willis to a husk, they spoke of what they had missed. Neither was religious, so there was no talk of meeting on the "other side". The grotesque disease brought them closer in a way their lives had not. Once, the son blurted," Dad, I love you." The old man coughed out, "I love you, too, son." Sometimes Jimmy sat holding his father's hand as he watched his labored breathing amid more frequent spasms of coughing.

One evening in December, after Bernice went to bed and Susan had gone home, Willis roused. "Son," he wheezed, "get me some water. How many pills do I have left?" His handkerchief caught the ragged, wet edge of a cough.

"They're right there beside you, Dad. I haven't kept track because the doctor gave us all we'll need. I'll get a glass."

When Jimmy returned, he glanced at the half full pill bottle. "Dad, you need to promise me you won't take too many. You know I asked the life insurance agent and the company won't pay if they can prove suicide. Mom's going to need that money."

"Yeah, I know. They make you suffer in order to collect. I won't OD, son, only enough." Willis took two tablets from the container, made out to swallow them, but kept them in his palm. He then lay back in the bed with a deep sigh and several coughs. He closed his eyes and was quickly snoring. Jimmy collected his lunch box and made for the door. He looked back at his father before leaving. The old man seemed at peace.

As Willis heard the pickup pulling back from the house, he looked up and swallowed. He counted out 20 of the pills, along with the two he had palmed. He figured there remained enough of the medication that no one would suspect his death was hastened. On his own terms, and with the last of his determination, he choked them down, two by two and leaned back. He trusted his pain would soon be gone forever.

****

The bedside clock displayed 4:38 am as Jimmy answered the phone. "He's gone," she sniffed. "He's so cold. I put a blanket over him."

"We'll be right there, Mom."

Susan rolled over as Jimmy went to the closet. Pulling on his jeans, he stuffed a small envelope in his front pocket.

"Has your dad passed?"

"Yeah. I'm going over now. Come when you can."

He saw his father's wasted body from the front door, in the same position as the night before except for the blanket. Bernice sat on the couch, staring vacantly. Sitting next to her he wrapped his arm around her shoulders.

"He was a good man," she said.

"Mom let's go in the kitchen and I'll fix some coffee. Susan will be here soon, and we need to decide what happens now."

With the percolator burbling on the counter and his mother at the table, Jimmy returned to the hospital bed. He absently brushed his father's sparse hair, and whispered, "I love you, Dad."

While Bernice was distracted, he pulled out the envelope. He emptied the cache of pills he had stockpiled into the few still in the bottle. No autopsy, no inquest, no investigation. He looked at his father's drawn face, straightened and went back to the kitchen.

The *Orion*

Located on the east side of Prince William Sound, Cordova, Alaska was organized in 1906 following the discovery of high-grade copper ore in nearby mountains. Unfortunately, a railroad and eventually a roadway constructed to extract the ore were wiped out by floods and landslides. A once thriving razor clam fishery was crippled by overfishing. The 1964 Good Friday earthquake raised the sea floor six feet and damaged the mussel beds. An important crab industry began to fall victim to the recovery of sea otters. The 1989 wreck and disastrous oil spill of the *Exxon Valdez* on the other side of the Sound devastated the herring and bait fisheries.

By 1998, Cordova was economically stagnant. Its only industry was commercial fishing for still-abundant salmon. A permanent population of between 2000 to 2500 people embraced and endured a summer incursion of sports fishermen, other tourists and employees for the canning plants, temporarily swelling the community to 3500 to 4000. During those long-day, summer months the added influx pressured the housing stock.

The Chamber of Commerce and other leaders frequently discussed economic diversification. In February 1998, they learned their counterparts in Yakutat, Valdez and Seward were promoting their communities as port-of-call cruise line stops.

Seward's glaciers and Ketchikan's extensive waterfront had been tourist destinations for years. The King Line in Seattle wanted to offer a cruise between those two cities to include Prince William Sound. Yakutat and Valdez were actively planning to join. A docking at Cordova with its stunning backdrop of the Chugach Mountains would nicely round out a tour package. The itinerary was set for the first arrival in June 1998.

****

The King Cruise Ship Line was founded in 1966 in Seattle, Washington. A small operation, its fleet of five ships for years plied a route featuring stops in Bellingham, Washington, and Victoria and Vancouver, British Columbia. The six-day "Honeymoon Cruise" added two additional days with a stop in Ketchikan, Alaska before returning to Seattle.

A regularly scheduled itinerary was often designed for a demographic, such as seniors. While there were no specific same-sex cruises, the King Line let it be known its ships were available for charter by anyone. For years their 100-passenger boat, the *Indigo Flyer*, was a favored charter by gay and lesbian groups.

Among *Indigo's* enthusiasts was Robert (Bob) Chandler, a tall, robust and successful lawyer in Seattle, who was the current president of the Front Runners Club, a thriving social organization for gay men. He and his partner, David Higgins, and others from the club had chartered trips on the Indigo. The cruise idea persisted but a change in scope and destinations appealed to him.

Cruise ship reservations were managed through travel agents. Chandler placed a call to his friend, Boris Vatten, owner of the Trade Winds Travel Agency two blocks down the street from his office.

"Boris, this is Bob Chandler. Do you have a few minutes?"

"Bob, my friend, I am always available to you."

"I'm calling about the Front Runner's Club annual excursion."

"Yes. Do you want me to explore dates for the *Indigo Flyer*?"

"I'm wondering about something bigger and a different itinerary."

"So, what's on your mind, Bob. What are you thinking?

"Well, what would it take to put together a trip with 500 passengers, a bigger ship and different ports-of-call?"

"Hmm. The number of people is probably a bigger challenge than the itinerary. How many members does your club have?"

"Only about 300 hundred, and not all would be interested at any price. So, I'd like to reach out to other places, like Portland or San Francisco. Do you have contacts in those cities?"

"As a matter of fact, I do. Your timing is fortuitous. I'd like to share something with you in person. Can you come by this afternoon?"

****

Over cocktails at home with his partner David, Bob gave full throat to his enthusiasm. He shared a copy of the e-mail bulletin received from Boris. The message was a travel agent recruitment for gay men's groups, couples or individuals offering a five-day cruise from Ketchikan to Seward, Alaska with three interim ports-of-call: Yakutat, Cordova and Valdez. At the Seward terminus, passengers would board a train to Anchorage for flights home. The King cruise liner *Orion* was available mid-June if at least 500 passengers were guaranteed. The larger the number signing on, the lower the individual cost.

The concept struck a responsive nerve throughout the Northwest. By late April 512 men had committed to the trip and paid deposits. Some were individuals, called by the beauty of the Southeast Alaska coast, while others were drawn by the social adventure. Couples came, too, young and older. Over 200 from the Front Runners Club and 26 members of Portland Centurion Glee Club were the largest groups. By June 14, they rallied in Ketchikan for departure on the *Orion* two days later.

The *Orion* was 445 feet long, 52 feet at the beam and drew about 40 feet. Twin engine diesels could sustain 21 knots. Four decks tall, featuring 300 cabins, most with seaward view, she could host 600 guests. In addition to the Captain, Purser, Engineer, Chief of Security and Chef, 100 other employees kept the ship afloat. Like all cruise liners, the *Orion* was at sea for days at a time, and a water making system was essential. The daily water needs of at least 600 people were too great for only on-board water. She relied on a Reverse Osmosis or RO system to propel sea water by high-pressure pump through mineral-stripping membranes.

****

At 5 pm, about an hour out from Cordova, Captain Robert Jenkins scanned the horizon from *Orion's* bridge. Medium in height, but broad in the beam, he wore King Line's standard beige shirt and navy-blue slacks. His name and rank were stenciled in gold letters about an inch high on his chest. Affable by nature, but stern when required, his crew respected him as level-headed and thoughtful. His white hair and beard contrasted with his weathered complexion. He had sailed around the world twice and had commanded vessels for 30 years. He planned for retirement early next year.

Engineer Bruce Hamner's tinny voice squawked from the overhead speaker, "Captain Jenkins, are you on the helm?" Use of the captain's rank and surname suggested concern.

"I'm in the bridge, Bruce, but Norm has the wheel. What's up?"

"Well, Captain, we have a problem. I'll join you in five minutes."

Jenkins and Hamner had sailed together many times. When the engineer eased through the bulkhead into the bridge, worry etched his face. He got right to the point.

"Captain, the high-pressure pump on the RO system is down."

Jenkins stiffened; his eyes narrowed.

"What do you mean 'down'? Don't we have a backup for that?"

"We have lots of membranes, but not the pump itself."

"Can you fix it on board, or would they have a replacement in Cordova?"

"We need to swap it out; the brushes are shot, and the coil is corroded. I think we need to call the Harbor Master. I doubt they have this pump in town, but he'll know who to call."

"How much water do we have left?"

"Not enough, Captain. "

"What about bottled water?"

"Captain, we all use about 100 gallons of water a day, not counting all that goes into food prep and clean-up. Quart bottles of water aren't going to cut it because we have to anchor offshore. This boat is going to be dry soon, and we can't leave these men on board."

"Bruce, you are saying we might have to spend tomorrow night in Cordova. We won't have enough water to keep the passengers on board. We're about to off-load 500 gay men in the morning and they'll need food, beds and bathrooms."

Minutes passed as the captain and engineer discussed their next moves. Norm, at the helm, silently watched the gauges.

The phone was answered in the Harbor Master's office almost immediately. James Roberts had directed maritime traffic in and out of Cordova for many years. It was unusual that he was still on duty after 5 PM but he was excited about the arrival of the community's first cruise ship. At the 60th parallel, the sun would not set until about 10:00. When Captain Jenkins identified himself, Roberts assumed he was calling for berthing instructions.

"Well, Mr. Roberts, we are going to need your help getting anchored, but we have a more immediate problem." After describing the equipment failure, Jenkins asked, "do you have an after-hours number for Western Marine in Anchorage?" An impressive array of contacts was a vital part of a harbor master's life. Roberts had just the number Jenkins needed.

"Thanks for your help. We'll call you in about an hour for mooring assistance."

****

Taking stock of their remaining supply, including the swimming pool, Jenkins and Hamner calculated they had enough fresh water to clean up breakfast. Sea water already served to flush toilets. After that, the boat would be dry until repaired. There was no practical way to bring potable water from shore. All passengers and most of the crew needed to disembark for town and would likely spend the night. That meant sharing the logistical crisis right away with their Cordova contacts. Jenkins mused about the information that would become the elephant in the room.

The primary connection with the Chamber of Commerce was Mary Kennedy, owner of the What Next Drive-Through Liquor Store. She had taken up operation when her husband died two years before. She had advocated for Cordova as a port-of call and planned to meet the *Orion* passengers at the foot of the loading dock.

Jenkins reached her at home. He told her of *Orion's* distress and that his entire manifest of passengers and crew likely had to remain in Cordova overnight. Mary surmised that the cafes and restaurants were already anticipating that number for lunch and could handle dinner as well. Accommodations for the night were a much larger challenge.

She asked, "How many passengers do you have? I've understood 500. We probably have about 50 vacant rooms in the motels. I'm stuck imagining space for at least 400 more with accommodations for couples, single folks and maybe some kids. Then there is the bathroom issue."

A long, pregnant pause prefaced Jenkins' careful reply.

"Well, Ms. Kennedy, the situation is both more and less complicated than you might think."

Another pause. A hint of dread rose in Mary's gut.

"My passengers are all male. This is a homosexual trip. They can all bunk together if that is what it takes. They need to go ashore first thing in the morning because we are going to run out of water. The company has given me the checkbook. We really need your help."

Mary's breathing went shallow. 'How did we not know?' she wondered.

****

Swelling strains of a closing chorus by Portland's Centurion Glee Club rounded out the formal dinner entertainment. Some long-term couples and newly minted others had already left for private quarters. But most of the passengers were still in the dining room when Captain Jenkins took the stage microphone.

"Good evening, gentlemen. I have an important announcement." When needed, Jenkins could affect a stentorian tone to command attention. He waited as the crowd slowly broke off their conversations and turned in his direction.

"As you know, we are about to arrive in Cordova, our second port of call. Without going into detail, I'm sorry to tell you that our on-board water making system has broken down. We have a reserve tank and the swimming pool which have about 5000 gallons of water, but that is not enough to reach Valdez. We have located a replacement motor in Anchorage, but it cannot be flown into Cordova until tomorrow afternoon at the earliest. We have a mechanic to install it, but then we need to run the unit for at least six hours to top off the tank. The bottom line is we will need to spend tomorrow night in Port."

Some passengers were all smiles, thinking the breakdown would be just another adventure. Others had a more sophisticated sense of the situation: without enough water on the ship, the passengers would spend the night in town, instead of cabins on-board. As president of the largest group on the passenger manifest, Bob Chandler had to ask:

"Captain, is there a chance we may have to stay on shore tomorrow night? Are you saying that if the unit doesn't work, or needs time to fill the tank, we're stuck here?"

"Mr. Chandler, we will do everything we can to get on our way and to stick with the itinerary. But I can't promise what I can't control. We are in contact with folks in town who are working on arrangements right now. By the end of breakfast tomorrow morning, we will share our plan. Naturally, the company will cover all expenses and reimburse your loss."

General grumbling swelled and then died down.

"All right everyone. Please enjoy the rest of your evening. In order to conserve our remaining water, feel free to use the toilets, please don't take showers. We arrive in Cordova soon and will moor north of town. Breakfast will be as usual, between 6 and 8 am. I will have more information for you by then. We want everyone to go ashore tomorrow and have fun."

By 6:30 PM *Orion* was securely anchored about a mile north of Cordova as the fishing boat harbor lacked enough draft. Owing to the 60° latitude, sundown was hours away. Passengers crowded the starboard side decks, staring in awe at the snow-capped Chugach Mountains surrounding town, capped by a brilliant blue sky. Seagulls screeched and banked, searching for handouts. Sea otters lazed on the surface, calling to their young, and breaking open dinner brought from the ocean floor. The breeze up the Sound carried varied aromas from the working marina.

****

Meanwhile, Mary Kennedy needed assistance and quickly. Within an hour most of the Chamber members were assembled in her dining room. The coffee pot burbled in the kitchen.

She silently rehearsed several ways to reveal the passengers' orientation. The mayor and six other men waited as she settled herself to open the discussion. She took a deep breath and began. First, she outlined the ship's predicament, necessitating the unloading of all 500 passengers. Then, she dived directly into the chaos.

When he heard "500 homosexual men" and "overnight" in the same sentence mayor Bill Boswell choked on his coffee. Russ Wilcox, owner of the Bait Bucket Sports Shack stared straight ahead, eyes bulging. Another scrutinized his shoes as he rocked back in his chair. Mary handed Boswell some napkins. Finally, the mayor asked what was on several minds, "Mary, did you know about this?"

Cordovans, like many Alaskans in remote, harsh areas were laconic, eccentric and libertarian. People did not move there for the social scene, but to be left to their own devices.

Ethnically diverse, socially conservative and self-reliant, they usually did not delve in their neighbors' affairs.

In 1998, few in Cordova talked about homosexuality; no one displayed it openly. There were covert relationships and discreet gatherings, but no same sex hands were held on the street. The few who were thought of as "different" were left to themselves. A heterosexual stereotype was the norm. For the next 24 hours, dramatic change in the form of 500 gay men would come up the gangway.

Stunned as the Chamber members were, and no matter what they felt about homosexuality, the visitors must be accommodated.

"Well, I hope these guys brought their wallets," offered the mayor, owner of the town's larger grocery store. "And, the fact is we invited them here."

Mary and her mates set to work.

A large space was required as a dormitory; the obvious choice was the high school gymnasium. Thankfully, the next day was Saturday, so students would be home.

Other vital concerns were cots, mattresses and bedding. Russ Wilcox lived next door to the Coast Guard station chief who offered his store of such essentials kept for drills and disasters. Mayor Boswell offered the three public works dump trucks to haul the supply. Calls to two local construction companies produced 14 porta-potties, which would supplement the boys' and girls' bathrooms in the gymnasium.

Breakfast the next morning was another conundrum. Most of the passengers and crew would be at the gymnasium; the restaurants and cafes that opened early would be overwhelmed by a concentrated onslaught of 500 hungry men.

The annual Cordova Iceworm Festival, usually held in February, had an organizational cadre headed by Mary's good friend, Marsha Bonine. Marsha was cooking dinner when Mary called and explained what was required. As was her nature, Marsha was blunt and direct:

"Let me wrap my mind around this: we will have 500 homosexual men hitting the harbor by 10 am tomorrow morning, and they can't go back to the ship until the next day? And then, you need someone to set up a breakfast line outside the gym for all of them, starting at 7 am? That means people, equipment and food. Some of my folks might not serve them. And, who the Hell is going to pay for it?"

After Marsha agreed to contact and organize her crew, Mary concluded the Chamber gathering. "We need to assign ourselves different parts of this plan to follow up. We can't just assume it will happen like clockwork tomorrow. Let's meet at the harbor at 8 am."

Wilcox spoke up, "I'll get the emergency walkie-talkies when I go over to the Coast Guard Station tonight. I'll hand them out first thing tomorrow."

****

During breakfast the next morning, the intercom carried the message throughout the *Orion:* a vital all-passenger and crew meeting was called for 8:30 am in the main dining room. Once the group assembled, Captain Jenkins again took the stage.

"Good morning, men. We have no choice other than to spend the night here in Cordova. There are some rooms confirmed in motels. With Mr. Chandler's help, we created a lottery to pick 48 of you. The rooms need to be double occupancy, so any man selected should choose a room partner.

We are told that the local eating establishments can serve us dinner as well as lunch. Ordinarily, you would be on your own for lunch, but the company has decided to cover both meals. So, keep your receipts, but you buy your own drinks.

The rest of you will bunk out in the high school gym. Each of you will have a cot and bedding. I will be joining you tonight since our engineer can supervise the repair.

Please arrive there by 9 pm so that we can get all of you settled. In fact, the town's volunteers could use help. We don't want someone staggering in at midnight, falling over in the dark. The next morning, before we depart, the city is arranging a breakfast line outside the gym. I know this is not the experience you anticipated in Cordova. But I give lots of credit to the city for putting together a plan in a matter of hours."

After Jenkins stood down, Bob Chandler and David his partner, were joined by Ken Adams, the leader of the Centurion Glee Club. As always, Ken was immaculately coifed and crisply dressed.

"Hey, I thought of something," Ken began. "What if we give a concert for the town to show our appreciation for what they are doing for us? I know my guys would be into it. We can use the same set we did last night. All we have to do is find a place and get the word out."

Bob and David stared and then nodded in agreement. Getting to his feet, Bob said,

"I'm going to find Jenkins and pitch the idea. Ken, I think you should come with me and we will approach him together."

After hearing Ken's plan, the captain placed another call to Mary Kennedy.

"I think it's great. I know the president of the Elks. They might let us use their meeting hall. I can print some flyers and get them distributed around town. They probably will charge something for the building, but they have a nice stage and a sound system."

Jenkins replied: "Mary, don't sweat the cost. If I can keep 500 men happy overnight, it will be well worth it. Oh, one more thing. I am coming ashore tomorrow morning, too. I plan to bunk down with the group in the gymnasium. Will anyone meet us at the harbor gangway?"

"The mayor, Bill Boswell and me, will be waiting to welcome you."

"That's great. I would like you, the mayor, and your spouses to join me for dinner. Your choice."

"That's thoughtful, Captain. I'm sure that Bill and his wife Joan will accept. I'm a widow so it will just me be me. We'll meet you in the morning."

Next morning dawned about 4 am. At 10, Mary and the mayor waited in bright sunshine as a line of *Orion's* launches made their way south to the boat harbor. The ferry dock was open, so several were able to tie up at once. Standing in the lead boat, Captain Jenkins' uniform displayed his rank and command.

Despite his size and near retirement age, Jenkins leaped onto the dock with a long-time sailor's ease. He confidently greeted Mary and mayor and again expressed appreciation for the town's efforts. He confirmed dinner with them for evening.

Mary reached into a bag and produced a 6-inch gold-painted wooden key. She said," Well, we intended to give you the key to the city. Maybe it should have been a key to the gym."

****

Robbie Minor was a native of Cordova, a graduate of the high school and a superb tenor. His job waiting tables at the Mountaineer Tavern didn't pay much, even with tips. But since he still lived at home with his parents his expenses were low. Shy by nature, he wasn't into the dating scene and largely kept to himself. Occasionally, he supplemented his gratuities by belting out a popular tune while serving Mountain Burgers and fries.

Like everyone else, Robbie was curious about the first-time arrival of a cruise ship. He was scheduled for a 10 to 6 shift, which meant salad prep followed by the lunch surge. Early afternoons could be slow. The sudden influx of several hundred people would mean significant all-day revenue for the Mountaineer and the rest of Cordova.

Among the first arrivals were ten passengers and the First Mate from the *Orion* who burst through the Mountaineer's double doors and made straight for the bar. Crowding stools two and three deep, they were an energy force. He immediately sensed their orientation as several men discreetly held hands under the tables. And, their members did not include any women.

During a round of Bloody Marys and two plates of nachos, one of the passenger-patrons learned of Robbie's singing talent. He wagered $50 Robbie could not pull off a credible version of Proud Mary. By the third verse, the passengers and other patrons were dancing in the aisles. The bet was won and the $50 in Robbie's wallet. Several of the group gave the him long, departing hugs. Since he was on duty until 6 pm, he declined their offers to join them for drinks. On the way out the First Mate asked the manager for Robbie's name.

Robbie was more curious than affronted by the same sex couples. Providing his best service came easily, including more songs, and the new patrons tipped him well. He felt appreciated for himself.

The first wave left, and others drifted in. Their numbers swarmed the waterfront and docks. Some tromped the marina passageways, fascinated by the variety of working fishing boats with their nets strewn everywhere. The pungent smell of day-old fish guts hung in the air. Kingfishers and gulls fussed and chattered, swooping and diving among the boats. Several harbor seals cruised the harbor like submarines with only noses out of the water. Boat captains and dock hands either looked the other way or stared in disbelief, shaking their heads.

Word spread quickly that *Orion's* passengers were all men. Some town folks came down to the waterfront to check them out, much like a traveling circus. Reactions varied. One local remarked to no one in particular, "Why, look at all those queers. There are hundreds of them and here they all are in Cordova."

As several smaller groups ambled along store fronts, a child shouted, "Mommy, those men are holding hands!"

Emma Rudolph turned off her "Open" sign and locked the door to her candy store. She wouldn't test her faith by serving "those kind". Other merchants, like the Eyak tribe, figured that their money would pay bills as well as any and threw out the welcome mat. In the Eyak Trading Post, an older couple admired a Copper River Fleece jacket, offered at a then unheard-of price of $75.

"Oh, Ron, you look so good in the blue one. You won't find this fancy embroidery anywhere else. Go ahead and buy it."

"Let's buy two. I won't want to share."

In fact, *Orion's* manifest spent freely, buying clothing, snacks, and trinkets, and eating and drinking with gusto. They had been given a rough map to guide them the three blocks to the high school gym.

About 4 pm, the First Mate returned to the Mountaineer and asked the afternoon manager for a chance to chat with

Robbie. He leaned in and asked whether Robbie had ever been to sea and if he would like an opportunity to see more of the outside world. Robbie's only excursions had been fishing in the Sound and a single trip to Anchorage. He learned that two crew members were leaving the *Orion,* and the boat needed another dining room server. Robbie already understood waiting tables and had clearly demonstrated his singing ability.

The offer was simple: he would join the cruise as a server until arrival in Seward. In addition to wages, and a share of the pre-paid tips, the company would put him on the ferry back to Cordova. He would be gone only four days and the manager could shift the Mountaineer schedules.

Robbie immediately agreed and after his shift went home to tell his parents. By then word had spread throughout town. His mother was worried about his "safety". His father's concern was more existential: was Robbie drawn to the "homosexual lifestyle?" Either way, it was clear he was leaving with the *Orion.* He changed clothes and headed to the Elks for the Centurion concert.

****

Mary's planning and the locals' efforts paid off. The passengers joined volunteers in arranging the gymnasium sleeping quarters. The biggest challenge was that darkness was not complete until after 11 pm. The Centurions were a huge success. Dressed in tuxedos, they sang without break for over an hour. Forty local folks gave them a standing ovation.

Captain Jenkins could have been excused from coming ashore by claiming the need to supervise the repair. But he decided to share the gym with his passengers. Hamner could see to the new motor. Instead, he joined Mary and the mayor and his wife at the Cannery for dinner. When they heard of his retirement plans, they regaled him with Cordova's virtues. They promised to join one another again at the ferry dock in the morning.

Dawn broke over the mountains above town about 4 am. Mary Bonine and the Iceworm Ladies began setting up the breakfast line. Early risers among the passengers carried propane tanks and stainless-steel chafing dishes into a row outside the gym. By 7, the enticing aromas of sausage and bacon wafted through the gym. Fried meats, scrambled eggs, toast, coffee, and juice rounded the menu. Other hundreds of hungry men needed no more of a wakeup call.

Most of the women working the mess line had no known experience with gay men. A few of Marsha's cadre refused to join. Those that did marveled at serving hundreds of them at one time, amid occasional whispers of, "Gosh, he's cute."

Mid-morning Jenkins again joined Mary at the dock. He was effusive in his praise and appreciation. She was thankful for dinner and drinks. He said," Mary, your town's hospitality under these circumstances tells me a lot about who lives here. I may take a further look about retirement."

He handed her an envelope that she later discovered held a check for a substantial sum, much more than their expenses. They embraced and Jenkins boarded the lead launch, headed north to the *Orion*. He waved and tipped his hat as the boat pulled into the main channel.

****

The decision to leave Cordova changed Robbie's life forever. By the time the *Orion* docked in Seward, he settled who he was and acknowledged what he had suppressed in himself. He opted to stay on board for the dead-head voyage back to Seattle. He began a career in the travel industry that sustained him for years. When he returned to Cordova months later, he brought his boyfriend, Aaron.

When the *Orion* departed the next morning, the local legend was born. Some recalled the roving clusters of men tromping on nets strewn on the docks. Others remembered fondly the impromptu concert performed by the Centurions. Still others hailed the town spirit that brought together the hot breakfast for the passengers who bedded down in the high school gym. All embraced the first cruise ship experience, and no later boat arrivals matched such challenge and reward for the community.

To this day, "…. *The town remains a community of independent, well-educated thinkers who are as diverse and as generous as can be found anywhere. It is a multi-cultural community of survivors who have weathered all the storms dealt to it, and with that, continue to survive.*" [Cathy

Sherman, Images of America, Cordova, Arcadia Publishing Library Edition, (2012), p. 127.]

Old Spot

After Lois Beasley and her husband Alvin moved to Calhoun County, she went looking for a new spiritual home. She attended Sunday service at the Mount Olive Evangelical Baptist Church outside Tinsman and felt right at home. Ever the social climber, Lois decided to invite the church leadership to a special dinner. Invitations were accepted from the pastor, choir director, church secretary and head deacon, as well as their spouses. She promised a rich beef stroganoff, topped by her specialty wild mushroom gravy.

Dinner was scheduled for Saturday afternoon and Lois began her preparations the day before. Because this was a gala event, she engaged Mrs. Richardson as a "helper lady". Women like Mrs. Richardson are found everywhere, supporting social events like Lois's soirée. Laconic in speech, they do what they are asked: prepping salad, setting the table, greeting the guests and showing them to the parlor. Helper Ladies become invisible when dinner begins.

Although Lois and Mrs. Richardson began early, the signature wild mushroom gravy was still to be prepared. With only a few hours remaining before the guests' arrival, Lois discovered to her dismay that the mushrooms she purchased from the Kroger in Camden had gone slimy. Her pantry stocked no canned mushrooms. None could be purchased in time for dinner.

Ever a practical man, Alvin suggested local stock. "Hon, there are mushrooms growing down in the pasture. Let me go collect some and see what you think."

"Oh, Alvin, I don't want to risk those mushrooms. I have always heard that some of them can make you very sick."

"But, honey, the best part of the stroganoff is the wild mushroom gravy. The dish won't be the same without it. I have an idea. I'll pick those mushrooms for you and you prepare some gravy. Then give it to old Spot the dog and we'll see what happens. If he doesn't get sick it should be fine for your guests."

Now desperate, Lois decided to try the experiment. She prepared gravy with the pasture's wild fungus and put some of it in Spot's bowl. The dog promptly wolfed down all the mixture, pushed the bowl around the kitchen floor and licked his chops. Expectantly, he looked up to ask for more. Lois was satisfied.

As Mrs. Richardson arranged the place settings and filled the water glasses, Lois saw to the final touches of the stroganoff and gravy. The guests arrived in good order and were shown into the parlor. After the usual small talk, they found their names on seating cards at the place settings. The customary blessing was offered by Reverend Sherman who went a bit over long for some of the hungry guests. At last, Grace was concluded, and the church brethren dug in with gusto. By general consensus the wild mushroom gravy was a complete success.

After the table was cleared, Lois was happily preparing dessert. Her favorable status with the church was assured. Just then Mrs. Richardson came to her side and whispered, "Missus, Spot's dead."

Lois gasped; her eyes bugged out. Ice water jolted through her panicked veins. "Oh, Lord," she murmured to herself, "I've poisoned them all." Visions of open casket funerals raced through her brain. Terrified, she grabbed the phone and called Doc Blanchard. Nearly hysterical, she described the circumstances. "Oh, Doctor, what am I going to do?"

Calm in the face of adversity, the country doctor offered his assurances.

"Don't worry Lois, I know just what to do. I'm coming right over. Keep everyone calm. When I get there, I will administer Ipecac and an enema. They won't feel so good, but I'm sure they will be fine."

True to his word, Blanchard arrived 10 minutes later and explained his intended treatment. Not wanting to risk a serious reaction, all took turns trooping into the bathroom.

Woozy, and much the worse for wear, they reassembled in the living room. Completely humiliated, Lois retreated to the kitchen. Looking at some of the wild mushroom gravy on the plates in the sink, she worried she would be banned from the church.

Just then, Mrs. Richardson re-entered the kitchen. She came to Lois' side. In her low voice she said, "Missus, when that fella ran over old Spot, he didn't even slow down".

The Phone Call

Henry Johnson laid the sports section on the dining table and picked up his coffee. The Giants had botched another close game in the ninth inning when the shortstop booted a routine ground ball. As he turned the page, his cell phone chimed. The number was unfamiliar; he opted not to answer, waiting for any message.

[click: Voice mail activated.]

After a few seconds, a younger woman's voice coughed, audibly inhaled, and said,

"Uh, Mr. Johnson, this is Hayley Stevens. You don't know me, but I really need to talk to you." A pause. "I'm calling about my mother, Doris Farmer. Please call me. I can be reached at 602-434-2109."

Henry stared out the window, transfixed in space. He replayed the message. 'Doris Farmer,' he thought. She had been a teller at the bank, petite, blue eyes, an easy smile. Though he was married, she had readily accepted his offer of lunch. More engagement followed. But after a few intimate times together, she was gone. Her colleagues at the bank had no information for him. He had heard nothing in the intervening 25 years. She would be in her mid-40s now, so Hayley was likely in her early 20s.

Though draped in dappled sunshine, Henry shivered. A plausible explanation was that Doris discovered she was pregnant and left town. If so, she had foregone any claim for support and raised her daughter on her own. And, if true, why was she seeking contact now? No other scenario seemed as likely. The possibilities were all troubled. Although unlisted, Hayley somehow learned his number.

Henry's default strategy for life's problems was to ignore them for as long as possible and hope for the best. Mental compartments made for better neighbors. With Hayley's number stashed in the desk drawer he returned to the sports section.

Few human challenges remain sequestered. They clamor for attention in direct proportion to their potential to upset life as known previously. Henry's thoughts returned often to the internal drama the phone call imposed. And, as predictably as night followed day, Hayley called again two days later.

This time she was more on edge. From Henry's phone prompt, she knew she had the correct number.

"Mr. Johnson, this is Hayley Stevens again. I know my earlier call was a surprise, but it's really important we talk." She inhaled twice. "My mother is very ill and is desperate to speak with you. Please, sir." She left the same number.

Alone at the dining table, Henry again considered his options. Ms. Stevens had shown her tenacity; this was important, she was not going away. If she had his number, she likely had his address as well. If he didn't call, she might show up on his doorstep unannounced. He retrieved the number from the drawer. Resigning himself he placed the call, picked up on the second ring.

"Hello?" came the same young voice.

"Hi, is this Hayley Stevens? This is Henry Johnson." An awkward silence followed. He heard her take a few deep breaths, as though steeling her resolve.

"Oh, Mr. Johnson, thank you so much for returning my call. I was afraid you would ignore me." She paused and Henry could hear her sit down. "Excuse me, sir, I am trying to compose my thoughts."

Henry was sure she had rehearsed these comments many times. This would not be some ad lib conversation.

"Sir, do you remember my mother? She worked at the bank where you were a customer."

"Yes, I remember her. A very nice person."

"Well, she told me you two were intimate, she became pregnant and I was the result. She said she wasn't with anyone else. I'm pretty sure you're my father."

The probable confirmation tightened his gut and cramped his breathing. He opted to admit nothing.

"Well, Ms. Stevens, I wouldn't know about that. You said your mother is ill and needs to speak to me. What's the situation? Where is she, what is she dealing with?"

"She is here in Clarkston, in a hospice facility. She has terminal cancer and they think she doesn't have much time."

"So, why does she need to see me? It sounds like nothing can be done for her. She didn't bother to contact me in the last quarter century."

"Please, sir, she made me promise not to tell you myself. She only wants a few minutes with you."

"What's the number, I can call her."

"Sir, it's her dying wish to see you one last time. I don't want to speak for her. Please come see her; it will mean so much."

Careening thoughts competed for his attention. He wrestled with how to shake loose from the call. Although it was only about an hour's drive away, nothing good could come from a visit to the facility.

"Well, I don't know, Ms. Stevens. It seems likely your mother wants me to do something and if I show up, she might think I've already agreed. What is it she wants?"

"Mr. Johnson, she desperately wants to tell you herself. I truly don't know for sure."

A few more seconds passed as Henry's mind raced.

"All right give me the number and address. I'm not saying I'm coming. I imagine I should call first." He wrote down the information.

"Thank you, sir. She doesn't have much time."

"Oh, and Hayley, I guess you can call me Henry or whatever. You don't need to address me as 'sir'. If I go see your mom, maybe we ought to get together, too."

"God bless you, sir, …. uh, Henry. ….. Dad."

****

The hospice facility was on the outskirts of town, set back off the main road. It was one of those non-descript, rambling, often remodeled buildings that had likely served a variety of institutional tenants. He found ample parking near the entrance. A help-wanted poster inside the left double door solicited smiling faces.

Behind the reception counter a thin, eager young woman with thick glasses and a headset looked up. Several groupings of overstuffed furniture in faded floral print filled the lobby. Two residents slumped near the door; one eyed him; the other saw nothing.

"Hello, can I help you?"

"Hi, I'm Henry Johnson. I'm here to see Doris Farmer. I called ahead."

"Yes, I think they are cleaning up after lunch. I'll call the floor nurse to see if Doris is ready."

Henry turned to scan his surroundings. Several tiled hallways branched out from reception. All were wide, with a handrail on each side. A wheelchair sat by a door; an IV trolley was down the way. A coffee maker and cups filled a small table by the desk.

Henry complied with the sign-in protocol and acknowledged this was his first visit.

"Are you family?"

"Not exactly."

"Well, Loren will be here soon to take you back. Do you want to have a seat while you wait? Or, a cup of coffee?"

Pouring a cup of dark, sludge-like brew, Henry stared out the window at the dusty landscape. Shortly, a tall platinum blonde came into reception from the right-hand hallway. "Mr. Johnson?" she asked.

"Hi, I'm Loren. Doris can see you now." She turned back as Henry fell in behind her. Most of the doorways were open. All had two beds separated by a curtain; some were occupied by shrunken figures. Others in pajamas and hospital gowns sat in chairs. Pinesol mixed with earthy odors hung in the air. The bright sunshine outside barely penetrated the gloom.

About eight doors down, Loren turned into their destination. Henry had bolstered himself. Doris was very ill and lung cancer is horribly unkind. Yet, even then he was shocked by her appearance. Her skull was covered with a light fuzz, the hair trying a comeback after chemotherapy. She was thin, pale, her eyes seeking to focus.

"Henry, is that you?"

Moving next to the bed, he took her cold hand. "Yeah, Doris, it's me."

"If you bring over the chair, I can see you better."

The hospital bed had the usual stainless-steel tray, with obligatory water bottle and flexible straw. Several pill bottles filled the space. Her breathing was labored and shallow, assisted by an oxygen tube and cannula. Though the room was warm, Doris had a blanket pulled up to her neck. Plastic flowers and a card rested on the window ledge.

Henry lugged the heavy chair from against the wall and positioned it near the middle of the bed. He retook her hand. The hospital bed was partially inclined. Doris tried to sit up straighter without success. Quiet settled as she composed herself.

In a soft, halting voice she said, "Henry, I know you have come a ways and Hayley said she didn't tell you why I needed to see you in person." She took several breaths.

"I'm really sad I never contacted you. You deserved to know about Hayley. But I knew you would never be with me, and I was afraid you would interfere, try to take her from me. So, I moved in with my mom when I found out I was pregnant, raised her and never called. I thank God you came to see me now."

"Well, Doris, Hayley was really vague, wouldn't tell me why we needed to meet in person. What is it I can do for you?"

"My time is almost over. I need to talk with you about Hayley. She's sick, too. She has kidney failure, probably from diabetes. She's been on dialysis for months."

Clarity began to dawn. Doris had not wanted to see him for herself.

"Henry, the treatment isn't working. Her counts are getting worse. My family has been tested and no one is a match for a transplant. I'm not eligible because of the cancer. She has been on a donor list for a long time, but the doctor says it could be years. You may be her only hope. I didn't want her to have to plead for her own life."

A kidney transplant: 'So, that's what this is about,', he thought. He did not feel tricked; there had been no deception. He did feel manipulated. And, afraid.

"Well, if her diabetes has damaged her own kidneys, wouldn't that happen to a transplant?" He was seeking a way out.

"We didn't get her on insulin soon enough. With a transplant, the doctors say she can lead a normal life."

"Doris, I've had no time to think about this. I just found out four days ago I have a daughter. I'm 56 years old. I can't give up one of my kidneys for someone I've never met."

"Henry, I understand this is sudden. But she doesn't have much time, either. Usually dialysis works better, but she has complications. She is retaining fluid and isn't processing toxins. Please go see her while you're here."

A cough caught her short of breath. She inhaled deeply into the oxygen supply.

"I won't keep you, Henry. I'm blessed you would come. I knew you were a good man at heart."

He squeezed her hand. With nothing more to be said, he walked out to his car. The September sky was hazy and indistinct. The afternoon was turning humid; the breeze had failed. The car's interior was stifling.

The ding-ding-ding of the car door alarm brought Henry from distant thoughts. He would not again see Doris Farmer.

Now, he was going to meet the daughter he did not know, who might need him in a way he could not have imagined.

****

The GPS displayed the map to Hayley's address, only a few minutes away. Now, he was the one rehearsing the direction of the conversation. Part of him wanted to run away, but the thought of driving home without meeting her was impossible. He called to confirm his arrival.

Swirling thoughts deflected his concentration. Each foray down a mental path soon diverted to something else. A car's horn behind him broke his reverie as a traffic light turned green.

Intrigued and intensely apprehensive, he found her apartment. The caffeine and nerves made his hands shake. Resolved, he walked up the sidewalk.

No one told him about the dog. When he rang the doorbell, a fierce cascade of high-pitched yelping revealed Hayley did not live alone.

"Trixie be quiet. It's all right, girl."

Yelping diminished to soft yips and rapid nail clicks on the linoleum. A dead bolt was thrown back, the door opened.

Each stared at the other across the threshold. Neither moved for a moment, taking in first impressions. Trixie came forward and sniffed his pant cuff.

"Hi. Thanks so much for coming. Please come in."

The apartment was small, sparsely furnished. Hayley sat in a chair, while Henry took the end of the couch. He looked older than she had expected. She was taller than her mother, with a sallow completion and puffy face. Trixie curled up next to her. A picture of Doris smiled from the side table.

"I've made some coffee. Would you like a cup? I know how dreadful the stuff is they brew at the facility. Do you take anything in it?"

She placed cups and saucers from the kitchen on the coffee table between them. Awkwardly they eyed one another, looking for common features and connection. He was struck by their resemblance.

Hayley dived in. "So, you saw my mom, she told you about my condition?"

"She did. She told me you're on dialysis. And that it isn't keeping up."

"I'm afraid I didn't get on insulin soon enough, and I wasn't very good at taking the injections as often as I should have."

Neither wanted to first introduce "transplant" into the conversation. Unusual in the initiative, Henry decided to lead.

"Doris told me your only hope is a transplant."

"Yeah, no one in her family is a suitable match. You might not be either." She had defined a simple resolution: find out if there is a match. If not, any moral obligation was satisfied. Of course, a favorable match would be the other side of the coin.

For a moment, Henry experienced an odd sensation: he spoke face to face with his daughter, while observing the conversation as though a third person from the side. Silence closed on the room. Henry held her eyes for a moment, then looked down. There was no doubting her ancestry; he was her father.

Yet, she was totally opaque. He would have passed her on the street without notice. And, now he could be asked to give her a functioning part of his body.

She handed him a business card. "If you decide to check our compatibility, here is the name of my specialist. She knows your name and has my permission to talk it over with you. I don't want to sound desperate, but she put my name on a registry weeks ago. We haven't heard anything, and my toxin counts are going up fast."

"Hayley, my head is spinning. I didn't know you existed until days ago. I just came from seeing your mother on her death bed. Now we've met and you may need one of my kidneys. I need time to think."

Understanding what was hoped for, if not expected, the conversation waned. They embraced at the door; Henry returned to his car.

She had told him of the match process and gave him the name of her nephrologist. He made no commitment to move forward but promised to be in touch.

The empty highway set his mind free. He drove on automatic, replaying the conversations. Doris rapidly faded; her life was over. Hayley, on the other hand, might still have a future.

****

In the two years since Diane left him for Margaret, Henry had retreated from the social scene. He should have seen it coming, he thought. He knew things weren't right, but to lose her to another woman? Diane would have no interest in the life struggles of his long-ago lover's child.

His only recurring social contact was with their daughter, Carrie, now a student at the university. Except for consoling her occasionally after various teenage crises, they seldom connected emotionally since. She understood her mother long before and always reminded him there was nothing he could have done. Carrie was levelheaded and calm, qualities he needed now.

She answered her cell phone right away. "Hi, Dad, what's happening? You don't usually call during the week."

"Yeah, I know. I need someone to talk to. Are you in class later today?"

"I'm free this afternoon. Are you in the car? When do you want to meet?"

"I'm on my way back from Clarkston. I'll be back in town about four. Can you come over then?" As inducement, he offered to pour them each a glass of wine.

****

Carrie was fit and willowy; to Henry's eye she resembled her half-sister despite the edema and pale complexion. She eyed him pensively and drew her legs up on the couch.

"So, Dad, what's goin' on? You haven't looked this wound up since you got the word from Mom."

He shifted in his seat, his rehearsed comments wooden and unsatisfactory.

"Carrie, I'm in shock. A lot has happened."

She said nothing, peering over her glass. Their eyes met.

"I got a call a few days ago from a young woman who said she is probably my daughter. I did have a brief affair with her mother over 20 years ago. Anyway, she told me her mother, Doris, is dying of cancer and insisted on seeing me one last time. Hayley, that's the daughter, wouldn't say why."

"That's why I was in Clarkston today, to see both of them. Doris told me that Hayley is also sick. She has kidney failure and is in trouble. After I left Doris, I went to meet Hayley in person. There is no question she is my daughter, and your sister."

Carrie's expression did not change, but she sat up straighter. She focused intently on her father. He looked down at his clasped hands.

'*Whatever is coming, it's big,*' she thought.

"Hon, Hayley needs a kidney transplant to survive. No one on that side is a match. Her mother is out because of her cancer. I may be her only hope."

Carrie stared at her father. He had just learned of a family he did not know. They did not contact him for concern, or even money; they sought a part of his existence.

Henry exhaled, spent emotionally. He concentrated on his hands as if they held the sought-for answer.

"What do they want you to do?"

"There is testing to learn whether I'm a suitable donor. The closer the match, the better chance for survival."

"Are you going to do it?"

"I don't know, hon. I just met this woman."

"Dad give me Hayley's number. I want to meet her, and soon."

****

"Hello?"

"Hi, is this Hayley? This is Carrie Johnson. I'm Henry's daughter from his marriage."

"Oh, my."

Seconds of silence were not awkward but were the beginning of their acquaintance.

"Hayley, my dad told me everything. I'm so sorry about your mom. And, you, too. How is she?"

"Well, thanks for asking. She took a bad turn after he left and may not last the week. I think she was holding on in hopes that he would come see her."

"I really want to meet you. Would you be willing?"

"Sure. I'd love to get together, too."

"I have classes today and tomorrow. Can we meet on Friday? I can drive over to Clarkston. What about lunch?"

****

They recognized one another immediately. Common interests, tastes, favorite celebrities and trends fueled conversation for nearly two hours. Neither had known about the other, but they chatted easily, sometimes pausing simply to look across the table.

"Did your mother ever tell you about dad? Did you know he was only an hour away?"

Hayley sighed. "She said she made a mistake getting together with a married man and didn't want to upset his other family. I think she was embarrassed that she hadn't taken any precautions. And, she figured he would insist on seeing me, would interfere with her boyfriends. On top of everything else mom got depressed and started drinking heavily. She was afraid he might try to take me. Grandma took care of us and said we didn't need him."

"Did you ask her about dad, what he was like?"

"I wanted to know everything about him, but she didn't really know him except physically. I pestered mom for years about contacting him, to let him know he had a child. After I was diagnosed and got worse, she gave in and told me about him."

"I can't imagine growing up without him. He is a good man."

Hayley looked away, staring into the distance. "Do you know what he's going to do?"

"Well, dad doesn't know it yet, but I'm going with him. We'll both be evaluated. I don't know if I'm a possible donor for you, but I want to find out. What if we are both eligible? Who decides?"

Meeting her eye, Hayley said, "I think I do. That's my understanding."

"All right, we're all in this together. One last thing, if either of us is a compatible donor, how would you pay for the transplant? That would cost a ton of money."

"Well, after I was born, my grandmother paid for a life insurance policy on my mother. She kept paying the premiums, so when mom dies, there will be some cash. And, when my kidneys failed, I was put on disability. That means I'm on Medicare."

"Oh, Hayley, I'm so glad we've met. I just wish it was under different circumstances. The three of us need to get together soon."

Hayley nodded slightly, acknowledging the generosity of newly met family. They parted with a hug and a promise to call.

Driving home, Carrie was struck by how quickly they had bonded.

I have a sister!

****

This time it was Carrie's turn to call Henry during the drive back from Clarkston.

"Dad."

"Yeah, hon, what is it?"

"Are you at home?"

"Carrie, this is the land line. Of course, I'm at home."

"I mean, are you going to be there? Don't go anywhere. I'll be about a half hour. You know I met Hayley today for lunch. We've so much to talk over."

"All right, I'll be here."

****

A week later, Henry, Hayley and Carrie were shown into Dr. Roberta Sanchez' office on the third floor of the hospital. Round-framed glasses pushed up on her head, she greeted them with a brief handshake. A green-tabbed chart sat in front of her. She smiled slightly, focusing on them before speaking.

"So, you're Hayley's father and half-sister. It's very generous of you to find out whether you are a suitable match for a transplant. Her mother's family is not in the picture. Donor kidneys are so hard to find I don't know if she has that much time. Her own kidneys are shut down. Dialysis usually keeps up, but Hayley has complications."

"What happens next?" Henry asked.

"It's fairly simple. We do a blood draw that tells us the extent of genetic match, your blood type and antibodies. We also do an environmental inventory. Even if you are a reasonable match, there may be reasons why you would not be a good candidate."

"Like what reasons?"

"The most common factors are high blood pressure, obesity and diabetes."

"Oh." Henry's eyes shifted upward.

"I have high blood pressure, but it's controlled by medication. I'm overweight, but not that much. My blood sugar tends to be high, but I don't think I'm diabetic."

Carrie said, "I'm in great shape. I don't have any of those issues." Hayley sat quietly, hands in her lap.

Sanchez continued, "The transplant process has become more sophisticated. We have anti-rejection drugs now that allow a much broader range of donors. Even without a perfect match, Hayley could live a long, productive life, probably have children."

"After the blood work, we'll meet again to review the results. Can you be available next week?"

****

When Carrie insisted joining Henry for the nephrologist's consultation, he thought she was just supportive. Now she was considering the donor's role, too. She was too young, he thought, her whole life ahead of her. Marriage, children, extended old age needed both kidneys. She might live for another 70 years.

As with her father, the last days had been an emotional whirlwind for Carrie. She had been thrown together with her father's sudden angst, discovering a sibling neither knew existed. Soon they would learn collectively whether the newest member of their family needed a precious gift from one of them.

Doris Farmer died the next day.

****

The blood work didn't take long. They sat again in the doctor's office. Bringing her glasses down from the top of her head, Sanchez studied the chart notes. She lifted her eyes to the small family across the desk and smiled broadly.

"Henry, Carrie, you are both potential donors. Dad, you are a closer genetic match. Carrie you are stronger on the environmental side. Hayley, have you spoken about who might be your choice?"

"We decided to wait until we knew the results. Do you have a recommendation?"

"Hayley, there are valid considerations each way. Your dad is a closer match. You would need less anti-rejection medications. Your sister's system is younger, closer to your age."

"I know this is momentous. Removal of a perfectly good kidney is a very big deal," said the doctor. "There is always risk in any surgery and we can't guarantee a result. I suggest you talk soon because Hayley's condition is worsening."

****

As they walked to the car, Henry asked, "Anyone hungry for Thai food? We could get some take out and eat at Hayley's place."

"Manola's is on the way. The apartment's a mess. You'll just have to deal with it."

They shared Pad Thai and pot stickers across the small dining room table. Trixie sniffed ankles, hoping for a tidbit. Plates cleared, they settled to talk about the path forward.

"Well," Henry said, "I want to share my thinking. I'm 56 years old. The time I have left is much shorter than you two. Carrie probably has 50 or 60 years more. She'll need both kidneys. Besides, I'm the one who caused this by being reckless with Doris."

"Dad, you know I love you. But, look at it this way. Your kidneys are 56 years old now. They weren't designed for the rest of your life, plus lots of years for Hayley. She needs a younger kidney. I'm ready to give her one of mine."

Hayley sat transfixed by their conversation. Logical, emotional, existential, they were discussing an essential organ as they might a used car. Henry and Carrie realized they were saying the same things several times. They looked to Hayley; she had begun weeping.

"I don't know how to express what I'm feeling," she said between sobs. "Two weeks ago, we didn't know one another. Now you're debating which one will be my donor. I can't tell you how much you mean to me."

Inhaling deeply and blowing her nose Hayley composed herself.

"I have thought about it, too, just as you have. I really don't want to ask this of either of you. I wish it would all go away. But, it won't."

"Dad, I know you said you were "reckless" with mom. I understand that. But, if you hadn't been with her, I wouldn't be here at all. Dr. Sanchez told me they are working on new drugs to extend life. If I need another transplant in the future, my chances will be better than now. I love you, Carrie, and I want you to live your life with both kidneys. If I need you in the future, I know you will be there for me."

Hayley inhaled, looking into her father's eyes.

"So, Dad, will you be my donor? Give me the gift of life a second time."

****

The muted glow of overhead fluorescents slowly illuminated Henry's consciousness. A voice was calling him from far away, but he could not discern the words. Time was indistinct, the surroundings blurry. He sensed the heated blanket warming his body and sought to remember where he was—and why.

"Dad, can you hear me? It's Carrie."

"My mouth's dry. Is there water?"

"I'll ask for a glass. How are you feeling?"

"Like I'm in a plane circling the airport but we aren't coming in for a landing. How long have I been out? Do we know how it's going with Hayley?" Henry was connected by an IV tube to a plastic bag above his head.

"You've been asleep for several hours. They took Hayley in about the same time as you. She had more prep work. I just heard that your kidney had blood flow right away, which is great. Now we wait awhile to find out if she is producing urine. So far, things look good."

The day after the surgeries, several amber drops were collected in a specimen cup. Hayley's color improved and her puffiness subsided.

Several weeks later, Henry, Hayley and Carrie found a table along the riverbank. A thermos of coffee and three cups ringed a small wooden box between them.

"My mom always liked this spot," Hayley offered. "The big maple trees were her favorite. When I asked her, she said she wanted her ashes spread here. I feel like she's with us, more than just in this box."

Henry said, "Well, Hayley, without that insurance policy we couldn't have done the operation. So, your mom was with us all."

Hayley picked up the container and walked down toward the river. She turned to her father and sister, opened the lid and tossed the ashes into the morning breeze. "Bye, mom. I love you."

An Agnostic's Journey

Frank Hudson was an original baby boomer, conceived a couple of months after V-J day. His parents were Caucasian, lower middle-class and predictably conventional. They attended the First Christian church, also known as the Disciples of Christ, in the small Midwestern town where he was born and raised. Although the community had a large minority population, the church was totally white. The only black person ever seen there was an elderly, blind gospel singer, brought in occasionally to break the tedium of usual worship.

He actively disliked Sunday services, which imposed an excruciating torture of boredom. Frank wanted to do something else – – anything else. His mother did not allow him to bring paper to draw on, let alone a book of his own. The only permitted reading choices where the Bible and hymnals mounted on the back of the next pew.

For a little kid, minutes stretched like hours. Sermons were the worst. Monotony eased near the end with passing of collection and communion plates. Frank wondered if these offerings came first as payment for the tiny glass of grape juice and cracker bits that followed. Upon conclusion of the service, Rev. Potter would stride up the aisle, gown flowing, buoyed by a rousing chorus of "Holy, Holy, Holy".

Like all religions, the Disciples knew the value of infusing their young early with the Holy Spirit. Sunday school came before regular service. Though he had no interest in the content, Frank envied those whose regular attendance was awarded by a badge, prominently displayed. For each new year of good attendance, they received a tiny, glazed add-on tab. They had status and Frank wanted to fit in. Yet the cost was too high. Frank's parents came to the church because of his mother's sister, Mary, the secretary. Among her duties were preparation of the communion plates and accounting of the offerings.

Ever socially conservative, Mary liked her steak well done and her bacon cremated. She quietly acknowledged a belief she had lived a previous life, showing potential rebellion below the surface.

Frank had no concrete sense of what it meant to be Christian. He knew that the Bible was the word of God, which offered the path to salvation and eternal life in Heaven, "the house of many rooms". God the father sent His son, Jesus, to live among us, return from the dead and lead us to salvation.

Yet, it was all abstract. Eventually, Frank understood there were versions of Christianity such as Methodist, Baptist, Lutheran, and so on; he had no idea how they differed. He couldn't say when he finally realized Catholics were also Christian.

Frank's mother had occasional spurts of religious fervor, such as when she sent him to a week of summer vacation Bible camp. He applied all the pleading and wheedling he could muster to avoid a second week's assault on his playtime.

As Frank entered his mid-teen years, he sought more responsibility and acceptance. One Sunday, without prior planning, in a fit of unexpected spiritual bonding, Frank went out the end of the pew, down the aisle and into the public embrace of the congregation. Disciples were not sprinkled at birth; instead, they came forward when they decided to declare their faith. Soon after, Rev. Potter dunked Frank and several others in the tank behind the pulpit. Officially, he was saved, initiated, and at peace.

In Frank's hometown during the 50s and 60s, there was little separation between the public schools and the Protestant religion. When he was in fifth grade, his teacher asked the class which church they attended. She assumed that each student had a church home.

In 1964, the year of Frank's graduation from high school, a "nativity" program was still presented. He was selected as the narrator, who introduced the various scenes. For Frank it was the perfect role, immersed in the conventional spiritual narrative while delivering the good word to all assembled.

Students portrayed the birth of Christ in the school auditorium, complete with Mary, Joseph, kneeling angels with candles, cut-out sheep and the Holy Spirit vision behind a gauze curtain.

No one questioned the concept of discussing Protestant religions in the elementary classroom or the presentation of a "nativity" program in the high school auditorium. The church and schools formed a protective, conventional umbrella overall.

Then Frank went to college.

For the first three years, his college life had no intersect with church or religion. His fraternity said grace before dinner, but that was the extent of overt religious observance. He offered no internal prayers or supplications. He became indifferent to the practice of religion.

Eventually, Frank began courting Karen, who became his first wife. She was a third-generation Norwegian farm girl from Northern Iowa, studying at the teachers' college near his hometown. A staunch Lutheran, Karen went to services, even in college.

Recognizing his spiritual lassitude, and to win the approval of her parents, Frank decided to join the Lutheran church. Study of the catechism and counseling with the pastor were requisites. Once you professed your acceptance of Luther's reliance on faith, you were good to go with life and the hereafter.

When Frank entered the role after confirmation, he was now a sworn-again Christian; he fit in. He and Karen never found a place for the lighted picture of Christ, a wedding gift from her grandmother.

Then he began law school. The fuzzy blur of the undergraduate curriculum sharpened toward a career. Frank was in his element. Assumptions were challenged, conclusions questioned. The purposes of the law were secular and concrete. The more erudite of his classmates put no trust in spiritual beliefs. Frank's recent conversion was under indirect attack.

Jonathan, one of Frank's Law Review cohorts was a confirmed believer. His father was a minister of some stripe and Jonathan an ardent adherent. One afternoon, he began to question Frank's convictions. When only limited tenets were acknowledged, Jonathan launched a full fundamentalist conversion monologue. It didn't take.

Frank hoped his colleague was correct for his sake. If he was mistaken about a critical point, Jonathon might end up in hell no matter his commitment. Frank later learned he came out as gay.

He wondered how the newly acknowledged orientation set with his classmate's father and his own conservative beliefs.

Frank never asked his aunt Mary about reincarnation. She once said she had lived as someone else, but he did not probe further. At her request, Frank agreed to divide and spread her ashes at the hometown church and his home in Oregon and Pacific Coast.

While tossing a portion of her remains in the church parking lot, Frank miscalculated the March wind's direction. Instead of sending her off with the stiff breeze, she deployed directly overhead – and onto his clothes and head. Mary had offered a lesson: even the best laid religious or ceremonial plans are fraught with the unknown or uncontrolled. She had the last laugh even from her next adventure.

****

Born in the high desert region east of the Cascades, Brian Smith was raised in a deeply conservative and religious ranch family. The fortunes of his parents' 640-acre cattle venture rose and fell with the weather and markets, both outside their control. When the spring rains nourished a strong grass forage, and the cattle thrived, they praised the Lord. If, instead, the cows were withered by drought, they cursed the devil. His folks reflexively sought refuge from the vicissitudes of life in prayer and scripture.

Some things were predictable: the ever-present tang of juniper in the air, the desiccated tumbleweeds skittering across the road in fall, and deep snow in winter. The wind could howl, swirl and drive the sand for hours at a time. Generally, though, ranch life brought much uncertainty, which could only be mitigated by hard work and God's grace.

His parents' faith was the beacon of their lives. They attended the Four-Square church, a faded, clapboard structure, plain as dirt. Preacher Jim was also the local mechanic who used the congregants' donations to fix the windows and buy a few hymnals. The year before last, church members accumulated enough materials and cash to install a bathroom in the rear.

Some, like Brian and his parents, came every Sunday. If someone new came through the door, he or she was greeted as a welcome, if unexpected guest. While officially Sunday was a day of rest, most everyone toiled every day. Bib overalls and aprons over smocks were common garb. All the men wore caps; most removed them during services. Bleached foreheads above sunburned cheeks gave testament to the unfiltered sun. They would return to chores or the kitchen after the benediction.

Strict adherents to their interpretation of the Bible, they found life's answers in both the Old and New Testaments. They believed in the Mark of the Beast, when the devil would come to take over the Earth, and the faithful would be called to Heaven in the Rapture. The pious would rally together for eternal life in the house of many rooms. Those couples living together without the benefit of marriage and practicing homosexuals were repugnant sinners, doomed to eternal suffering along with the non-believers.

Uncomplicated and certain, they knew and lived what they believed.

His parents brought baby Brian to Christening when he was only a few weeks old. He came to services as a toddler and attended church functions several times weekly. A blessing preceded every meal. Occasionally his father would be struck by a bolt of religious fervor and drop to his knees on the spot, head bowed, asking for guidance. They prayed together each night before bed.

This was Brian's life and he embraced it without question. His extended family, neighbors and friends held similar beliefs, insulating him from contrary views. He was mostly home-schooled by his mother which further kept his world view close to home.

Even as a teenager, he read scripture every day and could recite long passages from memory. One Sunday he was moved by the Holy Spirit to come forward for acceptance into the congregation. Soon after, the preacher baptized Brian and several others in the river. From his core he understood and accepted God's will as the guiding force of the universe. As he grew into adulthood, Brian embraced proselytizing. He accepted his duty to spread the word of God, to bring non-believers to the altar of sins' forgiveness and the promise of eternal life.

Over time, his religious certainty gave him self-confidence unusual for a young man with such limited exposure beyond his family. His unconscious knack for gaining empathy, even with those without faith, opened opportunities to probe for spiritual longings. His roughhewn, easy-going nature offered acceptance of others, even as he sought their conversion.

In the spring Brian turned 22, his mother's sister, Aunt Bertha called from Boise. She needed some brute force to refurbish her barn. Her husband had died, and her own son was stationed overseas in the army. She offered to pay for the plane ticket, if he would give her two weeks' effort. Naturally he agreed; he had never been out of state. His mother would drive him west over the pass to Eugene, Oregon for his first flight.

****

Frank's retirement from the legal profession gave him time to invest in the community. He ran successfully for the local school board. His logical bent gave him insight into the district's challenges. Managing public education policy required understanding the administration, teachers, classified staff, students, parents and general taxpayers. He accepted the board chair's request to attend a conference in Boise, to gain better understanding of new federal regulations about sex education. The trip was only an hour and a half by plane, rather than at least 10 by car.

Frank settled into a window seat with a book. A tall young man in a plaid shirt and Levi's took the aisle. They exchanged brief pleasantries as the jet taxied down the runway. Frank's seat mate bowed his head forward, eyes closed, hands clasped while the big plane thrust them back in its struggle to defy gravity. Airborne, Frank heard him exhale, "Amen."

"Your first time flying?"

"Yeah, and this will be my first time out of state."

"It should be an easy flight. The weather looks good, and we probably won't have turbulence." Frank returned to his novel.

"Do you fly often?"

"Well, from time to time. I didn't feel like driving all the way from Eugene."

The young man glanced past Frank and out the window. "Wow, the view from here is amazing, like you're looking down from heaven."

Once again, Frank settled in.

"I'm going to Boise to help my aunt; she needs a hand fixing up her barn."

Frank generally did not engage in plane flight chats unless he chose to initiate them. If a conversation took an unpleasant turn, there was nowhere to go. The young man's earnest reference to his trip's purpose seemed to offer bland interaction.

Frank weighed his choices. The novel in his lap had not yet engaged his interest. The young man beside him seemed likeable enough. His shirt, jeans and soft drawl suggested a rural background, which might prove interesting.

"It's nice of you to put in some labor for her."

"Well, scripture says to help others and she's my favorite aunt. By the way, I'm Brian."

"I'm Frank," shaking the outstretched hand.

The reference to the Bible put Frank on his guard. In very short order, his seat mate had introduced heaven, scripture and a welcoming hand. Many years had passed since he had any discussion about religion. Now was an unlikely time to re-enlist. He did not pursue further and went back to his reading.

Some minutes passed; Brian remained quiet, looking down on the Columbia River as the big plane hurtled east. Frank's concentration on the novel proved fickle. He closed it and put up the tray table. He reviewed his options: fend off more conversation to stare out the window or seek connection with his seat mate.

"I don't think I've met a young person who talks about scripture. Religion's pretty important to you?"

"Yeah, the Bible guides me every day. If something's bothering me, or I'm not sure what to do, God helps me find answers."

"That seems reassuring. Have you ever gone the wrong way, ever found you received bad advice?"

"Sure, I've made mistakes, but scripture is always correct. Sometimes I don't read it right."

Frank gave a short nod of understanding. "As I recall, some believe the Bible is the inspired word of God; they take it literally. Is that how it is for you?"

Brian sat up a bit straighter, seemed to brighten. Inquiry about his beliefs from an older stranger was energizing. Maybe God placed Frank next to him for a reason. He tempered his enthusiasm, not to come on too strongly.

"The Bible is God's word, given to us by His grace."

Frank began to rethink his inquiry. He checked his watch; they were about an hour out from Boise. Brian was clearly sizing him up as a potential conversion target, looking expectantly, urging some engagement.

"Well, Brian, I usually don't discuss religion with a believer because I don't accept it myself. I wouldn't want to insult your spiritual views." He reclined his seat the available three inches.

The pause in Brian's manner paralleled a slight downturn of his expression. Those he had approached before had not been so blunt. Maybe the devil sent him. Now Brian was on his guard; it might be well just to look out the window.

Each man pondered in silence. Frank wanted nothing to do with religious discourse, except as curiosity. How could someone think these things? For Brian the rejection was disappointing, that he had not reached Frank's longing for eternal answers.

Some minutes later, Frank brought up his seat back and hailed a cabin attendant for coffee. Changing his mind, he resolved to inquire further. Steeled with some caffeine he asked, "So, Brian, do you believe in evolution?"

"No, I don't. I think the world as it is now is how God created it."

"Do you have dogs on your ranch?"

"Sure do. Rex and Curly. They're good with the cattle."

"What breed are they?"

"Oh, they're kind of mixed."

"Quite a bit different than dachshunds, I guess," said Frank. "Do you accept that some in the Old Testament, like Methuselah, lived hundreds of years?"

"Yes, I think those peoples were very strong stock. That's how God made them."

"I guess that applies to Noah, too. I think he supposedly lived to 950. The Bible says he had two of everything, even things that creep. I wonder if he brought insects, like mosquitoes."

Brian replied, "Yes, I think he had them, too."

"So, did Noah bring just two dogs?"

"Frank, Genesis isn't specific, it just says 'every beast after his kind'."

"Hmmm. Brian there are some kinds of dog that didn't exist then. We've created new breeds by bringing different lines together to produce a new variety. Like dachshunds. Or, if a mixed-race couple has a child, that kid may not look like either parent. That sounds like evolution to me, just speeded up by humans."

"I believe in the Bible's teachings. We were made in God's image and not from apes."

"What do you make of fossils?"

"They were placed in the ground by Satan to test our faith."

Brian's placid recital caught Frank; unconsciously he leaned back. He had never heard such a claim.

"Is that in the Bible?"

"Satan is always trying to lead us away from God. If he can get us to doubt God's word, then he may capture us."

"So, how old do you believe the earth is?"

"The Bible isn't very specific about that. We think it's about 10 thousand years."

"Brian, there are scientific studies that use carbon isotopes to measure how old something is. They are studying things that are said to be many thousands of years old. Do you think the science is wrong?"

"I think they have assumed things that the Bible says are not true."

Frank looked out the window at the yellowing Eastern Washington bluffs.

"So, I imagine you think homosexuals are sinners, doomed to eternal suffering. Do you think that lifestyle is a choice, something they could turn off if they wanted?"

"Frank, the Bible is very clear that homos are blasphemers who are living their sin. It's unnatural, God did not make them that way. They could come to the Lord, but the devil has them captured."

"What do you think about gays and lesbians who are believers in God and worship as you do? Are they without hope because of who they love here on Earth?"

"They can't believe in the God of the Bible and fornicate together."

"I've heard that maybe ten percent of the population is homosexual. Many don't let that be known. Do you think any gay folks belong to your church?"

"There's no one like that in our church. We'd know for sure."

"Brian, what about peoples of other religions, like the Muslims. They have their own god, a prophet, a holy book. Are they consigned to hell, no matter how closely they follow their creed? I think some of them believe so strongly they are right, they would kill you for being a heretic."

"Frank, it's a satanic religion. He has his hold on them and will carry all of them to damnation, just like the gays."

"Do you think everyone has a soul? Maybe you can redeem it, even if you are a sinner."

"We're all sinners. But if you truly worship God, you can be redeemed."

"Do you believe in miracles? Is that how you accept things outside of our daily lives?"

"Sure. God's grace has been revealed by His miracles, especially the creation."

"Then, you believe in the Virgin Birth, the Resurrection and Heaven?"

"Frank, they are the proof of the Bible's teachings and our hope for salvation."

"Can you understand that for a non-believer that seems like fantasy?"

"Well, you have to allow God to enter your heart, and then you will believe."

Brian nodded slightly to himself and took the initiative. "Frank, what you choose about eternity is the most important decision you'll ever make."

Frank judged this was a line served up in many conversion initiatives. "I guess if you believe there is an eternity; I get your meaning."

Brian then asked, "Did you go to church as a kid? Have you read scripture?"

"Oh, I went to church with my folks, but religion never stuck with me. I finally decided it required me to believe what wasn't real."

"Do you believe in God?"

"Honestly, I don't."

"So, Frank, what do you think will happen when you die?"

Brian posed the existential question: is there life after death? If so, how do you get there? Does the Bible provide the answers?

Just then, the pilot announced the beginning of the plane's descent into Boise. Frank pushed the unread novel into his valise.

"Brian, I can tell how strongly you believe, but I don't share your acceptance of God or the Bible. I don't know what'll happen when I die, but I'm not going to the house with many rooms. It doesn't exist."

The plane landed hard and both men winced. At the gate they stood from their seats and gathered to leave. Brian said," Frank, I know you don't believe now, but it's never too late. Read John 3:16; it can give you some direction, some peace."

"Brian, good luck to you, as well. I hope for your sake you are on the right path."

****

Brian's aunt warmly embraced him in the airport lobby. On the drive out to her place, she asked about his first flight.

"It went pretty fast, Aunt Bertha. The guy next to me is an atheist and I tried to bring him to the Lord, but he has a heart of stone. He asked me some tough questions. I told him he should read some scripture, so maybe he can still see the light, but he doesn't believe."

"When we say devotions tonight, we can pray for his soul."

From the airport, Frank found lodging. His call home was quickly answered.

"Hello, love. It's good to hear your voice."

"Hey. How was your flight? How's the room?"

"This room could be anywhere. It's clean, though. Time in the air went quickly. I had an hour-long conversation with a young Christian believer. He was sizing me up for conversion."

"I'm surprised you engaged him. You usually avoid those folks."

"He was an interesting fellow. Easy going, very committed. He told me fossils were placed in the ground by the devil, to cast doubt on the Genesis story. He doesn't believe in evolution. He does accept miracles, at least the Christian ones."

"So, will you be going to services over there in Boise?"

"I don't think so. But the conversation got me thinking I want to update my advanced directive. I didn't buy into his plan for eternity, but I need to give more thought to this life's ending. And, I want to talk to Ed Peters about Death with Dignity. I need to review the provisions."

"Hon, are you feeling all right?"

"I feel fine. I just want to take another look."

"I know where to find that file. We can look them over when you get home."

Later that night, Frank reflected on the futility of discussing religion with a believer. Though next to each other, he and Brian spoke from alternative universes. Brian's acceptance of supernatural miracles put them on planes barely overlapping in the physical realm.

Frank entered life as a would-be fundamentalist Christian. His baptisms supposedly saved him forever. Now he accepted that he would leave purged of any religion. The journey had not been linear. Rather, his spiritual path veered, zigged and zagged, arrived nowhere. No divine plan, no awakening of faith, only ashes were certain.

Brian, a religious adherent, had a prescribed code of conduct. His God expected him to follow the tenets. In return, he was in the queue for eternal salvation. He could expect to join forever those who had gone before, whether he liked them or not.

Frank remained ill at ease. Religions require belief in other-worldly events, but he had no alternative explanation, no insurance policy. How did this world come about? What about belief in the Big Bang theory? What came before that? He fully embraced evolution but had no answers about eternity.

Though he had no settled story of creation, no religiously prescribed conduct, no promised heavenly life, he remained guided by respect for others and our increasingly fragile planet.

Following the call to do unto others as you would have them do unto you was a simple and complete moral code that required no outside intervention, no holy book, no rituals. Cherishing the Earth did not compel a belief in Genesis. Wherever the next adventure would take him, it would not be to the house of many rooms.

The Interrogation

Betty Kovaks rolled over on the first ring, checked the clock, and groaned.

'Damn, I just dropped off.'

Even before she had the phone to her ear, Sgt. Massey growled, "Are you awake Kovaks?"

"I am now, Sergeant, thank you. What's up?"

"Patrol just called in a body short on blood at 51267 Wildwood. The ME and a forensics team are rolling. There are a couple of uniforms on scene, but they need some help. What's your ETA?"

"Well, assuming I can roust Wheeler, we'll be there in about an hour."

Kovaks jotted down the address on the nightstand notebook; Wheeler's number was on speed dial.

"Mornin' Jeff," she replied to his foggy answer. "We have a body on Wildwood. I'll be in your driveway in a half hour."

"All in a days' work," he muttered.

Kovaks and Wheeler had been partners three years. They had a good close rate. She joined the department 12 years earlier as a jail matron. A woman then stood little chance of law enforcement advancement in rural Arkansas. Betty persevered, outlasted two changes of sheriff and became the first sworn woman officer. Not long after, she became the first female detective.

She was intuitive, keen to the sometimes-subtle triggers that spark action. Her empathy garnered trust despite the badge.

Jeff Wheeler graduated from the local high school and the University. His degree gave him a leg up for department requirements. She was the lead. He was the note taker, the background checker, the one who challenged their first take.

They stopped by a twenty-four-hour donut shop on the way to the crime scene; it would be a long day. The Wildwood address was a down-at-the heels bungalow with a sagging fence and yellow crime scene ribbon across the gate. A patrol car occupied the driveway. A gray Crown Vic with trunk open was at the curb. As they parked across the street, one of the uniformed officers left the black and white to meet them.

"Morning, Officer Jensen, what have we got here?"

"Well, it looks straightforward right now. I left Officer Curtis at the crime scene and went over to interview the neighbor who called it in. He is Robert Eugene Thomas, DOB 7/2/46, they have lived here for 15 years. His wife heard a gunshot about an hour ago. She rousted Mr. Thomas who came over with a flashlight and his cell phone. The door was ajar, so he stepped in and found the victim on the floor. It didn't take much to deduce he died from a gunshot wound, so he called the department."

Wheeler jotted down some notes. "Okay, what have you done so far?"

"We got here at 2:23 am and found the victim just as Thomas described. We secured the residence, called for you guys and the ME. Like I said, I went over and interviewed Mr. Thomas. Several other neighbors came out to gawk, but I've kept them away from the house. Then I set up a crime scene log. That's about it."

"Hey, you guys did great. Let us sign in. We'll get booties from the car."

The house was now brightly lit, several figures moved purposefully inside. From the front door, Kovacs and Wheeler assessed the living room. The body was face down on the floor with an obvious exit wound in back. The pool of blood from under the chest confirmed he was no longer living. Pizza boxes piled on the coffee table and kitchen floor. Beer bottles accumulated in several locations. The house held an obvious after-party aroma.

The chief lab technician, John Brewster, joined them.

"What have you got for us, John?"

"Well, we haven't moved the body. You can see it's a through and through gunshot that was immediately fatal. Of course, we don't know for sure, this doesn't look like a robbery. The victim's wallet is on his dresser with over $200 and his cell phone is on the table. His laptop is still on the desk. Nothing has been ransacked, no signs of struggle or forced entry. So far, we haven't found a shell casing. Either the shooter used a revolver, or picked up the brass."

"John, you said the wallet's still here. Is there a driver's license? You think this is our victim?"

"The license is issued to Travis Eugene Morgan, DOB 4/14/98. We haven't done the fingerprint comparison yet, but I'd say this is Travis."

Another of the techs joined them.

"Detectives, I have three things so far. We found the bullet in the wall across from the front door. The autopsy could tell us the bullet's trajectory through the body. From where bullet struck the wall, back through the body, might give us an idea how far off floor the gun was. And, that may give us some sense about the size of the shooter. Of course, the trajectory could be off, depending on what the bullet struck on its way through the body."

"Okay, that's a start. What else do you have?"

"We decided to put the kitchen garbage in its own evidence bag. Before we closed it, though, we found this." Between his gloved finger and thumb he held a short, red straw. "On this end is what looks like white drug residue. We'll take it to the lab, but I wager we'll find either coke or meth."

"Have you looked at his cell phone yet?"

"No, we decided to leave that for you. We dusted it for prints and have photographs. You can look it over if you want."

"So, what's the third thing you have for us?"

The tech handed Kovacs another clear evidence bag. It held a light pink brassiere. "We found this outside by the sidewalk. We'll look at it for DNA or fibers. The tag says 34B."

Wheeler asked, "do you have a picture of where you found this? You said along the sidewalk."

"Yeah, we have lots of pics. It was about halfway between the front door and the gate to the street."

"Well, thanks. We'll see what we can make of it."

Outside Kovaks mused on how little they knew. "At least we're pretty sure who the victim is, and about when he was shot. Other than that, we have no idea by whom and why. You go talk to the neighbor; I'll look at the cell phone."

****

With Officer Jensen in tow, Wheeler crossed to Thomas' front door. The lights were still on and he answered right away. His eyes were bright as he ushered them in.

Wheeler thought, *'This is his only moment in the sun, part of a murder investigation'.*

After introductions by Officer Jensen, Thomas readily agreed to tell all he knew, and a recording was made.

"I sleep pretty sound, and I take my hearing aids out. And, I had two glasses of wine before bed. So, I didn't hear anything myself. Marion started shaking me and told me she heard a gunshot next door. I was groggy, but I couldn't imagine someone shooting a gun in our neighborhood. Anyway, Marion was insistent and made me go to Travis' place. To stay in touch, I called her cell phone from mine and carried a flashlight. I kept telling her what I saw as I went to the front door. The house was totally dark except for the streetlight at the corner. After I came on the porch, I could see the door was part way open. I pushed it aside and stepped in. Right off I saw him on the floor. I'm sure I blurted out something like *'oh my god'*. Marion became hysterical and crying. So, I called you guys right away."

Wheeler inquired whether he had moved around inside or touched anything.

"No, I wanted to get out of there. My neighbor was gunned down, right next door. I backed out and went to be with Marion."

"Speaking of your wife, is she here? I'd like to get her statement, too."

"Well, detective, after she found out that young Travis had been murdered just across the fence, she took a Xanax and an Ambien. She won't be available for several hours."

****

Travis Morgan's cell phone had basic features, including a contact list and voice mail. It held two messages.

[Metallic click: "Friday, 4:38 pm:"]

'Hey, Travis, Carl here. Sorry dude, but I can't make it to your place tonight. Someone called in sick, so I have to take the shift. Let me know about the next one. Thanks, Bud.'

[Another click: "Saturday, 1:31 am:"]

'Hi, Travis, it's Brenda. Listen I know it's late, but I'm pretty sure I left my bra at your place. Remember when you were giving me a back rub? I had a drink too many after that. I'll call you later about coming over.'

The contacts did not reveal Carl, but Brenda Avery's address and phone number were listed. Betty Kovaks noted the contact information.

****

The detectives met outside and shared developments. Kovaks said, "From the cell phone I have a line on a woman who was here last night and left the bra. Her name is Brenda Avery. Let's go see her now, bring her to the office."

Next door, the lights and camera from a TV station heralded the arrival of the press. In the glow stood Mr. Thomas, extending his moment of fame for the morning news cycle. It was only a matter of time before reporters began peppering the department for information.

Brenda Avery lived in an apartment complex about 10 minutes from Travis' home. The detectives stepped onto her porch and rang the bell. After about 30 seconds, Wheeler began banging hard on the entrance.

"Ms. Avery, this is Detective Jeff Wheeler from the Sheriff's Office. We really need to talk to you. Please come to the door."

Shortly, a light came on inside, accompanied by movement near the door. A shadow passed across the peep hole, followed by the porch light. Satisfied they posed no harm, Brenda Avery opened the door.

Dressed in her robe, she blinked several times, trying to decipher the scene in front of her.

"Are you Brenda Avery? I'm Detective Kovaks, this is Detective Wheeler. We are conducting an investigation about Travis Morgan. You know him?"

"Yeah, I was just at his house. I've only been home for a couple of hours. What's going on? Is he OK?"

She looked from one to the other, searching their eyes.

"Well, Ms. Avery, we don't know very much yet, and we need your help. We'd like you to come to the office with us. It probably won't take long. We can check on things easier if we work from there."

"But, can't we talk here? I have to work this afternoon."

"I know you want to help us, Brenda, and I promise you'll be back here in time for work."

The Sheriff's Office was a sprawling array of mismatched additions, topped with antennae and communication devises. Police vehicles parked on all sides.

Although September was still warm, Brenda shivered as she sat alone in the bare interview room. It was like an oversized closet, with only a door and a mirrored window. A steel table with mounted eye bolt was surrounded by three metal frame chairs with cracked seat cushions.

'Why won't they tell me anything? Is Travis hurt? Is someone missing?'

The detectives discussed how to conduct the questioning. To Kovaks, she seemed troubled by the unknown, rather than frantic about what might be revealed. They would give as little information as possible. Kovaks would begin alone, with Wheeler behind the mirror with the recorder.

They needed a list of everyone at the house that night and to learn her connection to the deceased. They knew she had taken her shirt and bra off to enjoy a backrub from him. Someone was likely snorting a white drug; did she see the straw in use? More questions would flow from her answers.

Kovaks entered the room carrying two Styrofoam cups of dark liquid.

"Ok, Brenda, thanks for waiting. First, I want you to know a tape recording is being made of our conversation. Are you speaking with me voluntarily?"

"Uh, yeah. But I don't know what's going on."

"Just a moment, Brenda, I have to note some things: This is Detective Betty Kovaks, Fremont County Sheriff's Office, it's 3:15 am, September 12, I'm speaking with Brenda Avery, DOB 5/23/97."

"Brenda, we will get to your questions, too, but let me get some information first."

Kovaks was encouraging, offering an open face. In short order Brenda related she had known Travis Morgan since high school. They had not dated, but she liked him as approachable. Her recollection of the others at the house included her sometime boyfriend, Charlie Fisher. Another young couple left before Brenda.

The detective asked if anything unusual had happened. Brenda looked down. "I left my bra over there. Travis offered to give me a back massage. I think I forgot to put it back on. I was pretty wasted when I went home."

Then she looked up, "So that's how you found me so fast. My message on his cell phone. You've got to tell me what's wrong. I'm getting scared."

"Brenda, I think you've been honest with me, so I'm going to share some things with you. There are lots we don't know yet, but I'm sorry to tell you Travis is dead. He was shot in his living room. We're trying to figure out who did it."

Brenda's jaw began to drop, and tears flowed. "No, no, no. I was just with him a few hours ago. He was a great guy. Who would do such a thing?" She cried hard. Gulping a few times she slowly regained her composure.

"Oh, god, oh, god, this is horrible." She looked up, took several deep breaths and blew her nose. "Someone shot him in his own home?"

"So, the other couple, you said they are David and Cassie, left before you did? What about Charlie?"

"He insisted he take me home. I'm glad he did because I was drunk by then."

"You were alone when we picked you up. Did Charlie want to stay the night?"

'There's something going on here,' Kovaks mused.

"I've been trying to cool his jets about me. He's just too controlling, so I told him I didn't feel good. He didn't like it, but he left after dropping me off."

"So, you and Charlie have been intimate, but you weren't interested tonight?"

"The problem is that he thinks we're a couple, but I don't. He's not that interesting."

"Did he know about the back massage? Was this in the living room or Travis' bedroom?"

"I don't remember for certain, but I think in his room. Like I said, I was drinking a lot."

"My partner just texted me Charlie's address. Does 1066 Byron Street sound right?"

"Yeah, that's it."

"So, that's only about 10 minutes from Wildwood, correct? What time did he drop you off?"

"I don't know. Maybe about 1 am?"

"OK, Brenda, tell me what else happened at Travis' place. There was a lot of marijuana and paraphernalia, along with plenty of beer bottles. We don't care about that stuff."

"Well, I don't know what you mean."

'I'll let that sit for a minute before I move on. She's going to have to say something.'

Brenda slightly nodded her head as though she had reached resolve.

"I think the other boy, David, and Charlie were snorting some white drug. Knowing Charlie, if he brought it, it was meth."

"Where did they do that?"

"They were doing it in the kitchen. I think Cassie got pissed off that David was snorting. They left right after that."

"Did Travis have conflict with anyone that night?"

"Not really. I know that Charlie didn't like the massage thing. I think we left the door open so it didn't look like we were hiding out. Where was my bra?"

"Out along the sidewalk. Any idea how it got there?"

"Not for sure. I guess I brought home a box with cold pizza because it's in my kitchen. I probably had my hands full and dropped the bra on the way out to Charlie's car."

"You told me Charlie's not interesting to you. What is he into, what does he do with his time?"

"I didn't know him well in high school. He was into hunting. If you walked past him in the fall, he would be going on about opening deer season, cleaning his rifle, that kind of thing."

'Let's dig in here. What is she going to tell me?'

"Did he ever want to show you his guns?"

"Only once. He brought out his rifle from the closet. It had a scope, and he told me he used it for shooting deer."

On a hunch, Kovaks asked, "Any other guns?"

Brenda began her answer, then caught herself. She was mentally evaluating something.

"Do you think Travis was killed with a rifle?"

"Probably not. A long gun bullet would have likely gone completely through the house. Instead, we found it in the opposite wall. It looks like he was killed by a handgun."

'She wants to tell me something. Maybe Charlie also has a pistol.'

"I asked you about other guns and you started to tell me something. What was it?"

"Brenda fiddled with the hanky in her lap, looked to the side, then down again.

"Charlie has a handgun, too."

'Bingo.'

The detective's radar counselled caution, not to seem too eager.

"What kind is it? Do you know the difference between a revolver and a semi-automatic?"

"It's a revolver. The difference is about all I know."

"When did you see it? Was it at his place on Byron?"

"Yeah. I was over there for my birthday, August 30. He had the rifle in a case in the closet and the handgun was wrapped in a cloth in his top dresser drawer."

"Did he tell how he got it? Or, why?"

"He said he got it through a guy at the packing plant. He said the gun gave him a lift, that he could better take care of himself. That's a big part of why I don't want to hang out with him. I don't like guns."

"Any idea how big it was, the caliber?"

"No, I don't."

"Has he told you whether he still has it? Any indication he disposed of it?"

"He never said more about it."

After some follow up questions Kovaks said, "Brenda, part of an investigation is eliminating people as suspects, as well as trying to identify those who could be involved. I want to do a swab of your hands for gunpowder residue. Do you have any problem with that?"

****

After taking Brenda Avery back to her apartment, Kovaks and Wheeler reviewed their notes.

"I don't think she's the shooter. Either that or she should get an Academy Award. We need to talk to Charlie Fisher right away. Let's show up, like we did with Brenda, not give him warning."

Wheeler nodded his agreement. It was now about 5 am, so they stopped for breakfast. As they headed back to their unmarked, she received a text: "Hi, Detective Kovaks. This is Darren Small from KMMY. We would like your comments on Travis Morgan's murder. Have you notified the next of kin?"

"Mr. Thomas wasn't shy about identifying the victim. The body is barely cool and the press is circling already. I'll deal with this when we get to the office."

Charlie Fisher lived in a duplex on the corner. A lifted pick-up with giant tires sat in the driveway. The porch light was on, the residence was dark.

"Mr. Fisher, we're from the Sheriff's Office. We need to talk to you right now." Wheeler struck the door hard and often. "Mr. Fisher, come out now!"

Muffled sounds of movement came closer. A piece of furniture tipped over. "Jeezus, what the hell is this?"

The door opened and a dazed looking Charlie Fisher stood framed by the porch light.

"What the fuck is going on?" he growled, squinting at the two figures on the landing. Kovaks held a Kel-lite, focused on Fisher's torso. Badge wallets were displayed in his direction.

"Are you Charlie Fisher? We're detectives Kovaks and Wheeler from the Sheriff's Office. May we come in?"

Fisher swayed slightly, trying to comprehend. Then the words "detectives" and "Sheriff's Office" began to gel. He looked from one to the other and said, "What do you want?"

"Sir, we're conducting an investigation and we need to talk with you. Can we come in?" At 6' 2", Wheeler usually led these confrontations.

Charlie was in the boxer shorts and T-shirt he wore to bed. He backed up a few paces and they moved past him.

"Mr. Fisher, I'll take you into your bedroom, because we need you to get dressed." Wheeler was directive, in control. From here on, Fisher would not be out of their sight.

Kovaks scanned the room. This moment was key: they had no grounds to arrest Fisher. They acutely needed to interview him at their office, not the comfort of his living room. Yet, if he refused to accompany them, they were stuck.

"What's this about? What's goin' on?"

"Sir, we are investigating circumstances about Travis Morgan. We understand you were with him earlier today. We need to learn what you know so we can figure it out."

"I didn't do anything wrong. Why are you hassling me?"

"Please, Mr. Fisher, get some pants on. No one is accusing you of anything. But we have a situation to deal with and we need to know if you can help us."

About 20 minutes later, Charlie Fisher sat in the same interview room as had Brenda Avery. Again, the detectives commiserated outside, evaluating their approach.

Turning to Kovaks, Wheeler asked, "Well, Betty, do you like this guy? He was there, he owns a handgun and his girlfriend was in the victim's bedroom with her shirt off. And, he was doing some white drug."

"I don't know. You're usually the one to poke holes. How do you want to go at him?"

"What do we have from the lab? I think we tell him his fingerprints are on the straw. This guy doesn't have the juice for coke, so we tell him we know it's meth. I think we surprise him with the bra and see what we think about the gun. Let's start together and see what happens," Wheeler said. "We may not get the truth, but maybe he'll tell so many lies we can get him that way. By the way the lab left a message: the weapon was a .32. We don't have fingerprints for Fisher, but there are some good ridges on the straw. Did you see his eyes?"

"Yeah, I did. But, let's leave open he didn't pull the trigger. You take the lead."

They glanced through the mirrored window. Charlie Fisher sat bewildered. Hair stuck out in all directions; stubble darkened his chin and cheeks; his eyes were bloodshot, pupils dilated.

As with Brenda, they brought in a cup of department coffee. An oily sheen discouraged consumption.

"All right, Mr. Fisher, hopefully this won't take long. You are not in custody; you can go anytime. We're going to record our conversation so we all know what was said. You OK with that?"

"I didn't do anything. What's going on?"

Kovaks eyed Fisher intently. *'We told him we're investigating about his friend, Travis Morgan, but he hasn't asked about him. Maybe it's because he knows what happened.'*

"How do you know Travis Morgan?" Wheeler began controlling the flow of information, assuming the acquaintanceship.

"We went to high school together. We were in lots of the same classes. He's a great guy."

It seemed to dawn on Fisher he ought to express concern.

"Hey, is Travis in trouble? Is he hurt?"

Wheeler was not ready to acknowledge Travis' murder.

"We understand you were over at his place last night, correct? Who else was there?"

Fisher nodded to himself, began rubbing his hands together and moved around in the hard chair. His focus was irregular, his mind unsettled, his breathing shallow.

"I asked you who else was at Travis' house."

"Uh, there was a couple I didn't know, David and Cassie. I didn't get their last names. Brenda Avery was there." Kovaks made notations.

"We were at Travis' place a few hours ago, and there was marijuana all over. Who brought the weed?"

"I brought a little bit and I think David had some, too. Everybody had a toke or two. I mean, who doesn't these days?"

"Any other drugs there?"

"Not that I remember, but I got pretty drunk. I'm still hungover."

"What do you know about this?" From a file folder Wheeler handed him a picture of the red straw on top of the garbage.

Charlie Fisher stared at the photo as if it was a winning lottery ticket. "Huh. Yeah, it's coming back to me. David brought some white dope and he used the straw to snort it."

"Whose fingerprints might be on that straw? Did you use any?"

Fisher was no genius. Yet he was street-smart shrewd. He guessed the authorities couldn't raise an identifiable print on that thin piece of plastic.

"Can't say. I don't remember. I don't think so."

Wheeler sat back in his chair, a cue for Kovaks if she wanted.

"Mr. Fisher," she asked, "tell us about your relationship with Brenda Avery."

"I've known her for years. We went to school together, too. We've dated some."

"Is she your girlfriend?"

Fisher had not again asked about Travis. Kovaks mused to herself, *'This guy is really on edge.'*

"Well, I wanted us to be together. But after a few dates she started pushing me away. She said I was too controlling. I just wanted her to know I cared."

"Is she dating anyone else?"

Fisher raised his head, squinting at them. "What the hell is going on? Why are you asking me all this? Why won't you tell me about Travis?"

"Mr. Fisher, Travis Morgan is dead. He was shot in his living room; we think about five hours ago. You were one of the last people to see him alive, so we're trying find out what happened."

"Whoa, hold on. I didn't do anything. He was fine when I took Brenda home, about 1 am." He held his palms toward the detectives as though fending off the thought of his involvement.

Wheeler took over. "What do you know about this?" From the same file he slid across a picture of the pink bra by the sidewalk.

By now Charlie Fisher concluded the authorities had interviewed Brenda. Since Cassie left earlier, Brenda was the only source.

"I know Brenda has a pink one like that. Is it hers?" Fisher was not subtle; he desperately wanted to mine the detectives' information. What did they know, what could he use for himself?

"What size does she wear?" Kovaks asked.

Fisher blinked twice and looked up as if searching the ceiling for the answer.

'He's been intimate with her. He has to know the answer, but he's worried.'

"I don't remember for sure. She's kind of small, so probably a B cup."

"Any idea how the bra ended up outside by the sidewalk?"

"Well, I glanced in Travis' bedroom once, and he was giving her a back rub. She was bare to the waist, so I guess that's how it came off. I don't know after that."

"Did that bother you, your girlfriend in your buddy's bedroom bare chested?"

Fisher's reply came too quickly and seemed forced. "The door was open, and he had his clothes on."

'Now we're getting somewhere. The backrub pissed him off a lot.'

"Do you enjoy hunting?" The question caught Fisher off guard.

"Sure, lots of guys like me go deer hunting. The season is coming up later this month. I got my tags last week." Charlie was becoming anxious and hoped his commentary would mitigate his interest in guns.

"Brenda told us you have a rifle with a scope."

"Yeah, it's a Ruger 30-06 and the scope is 4 X 20."

'So, he knows the brand, caliber and scope specs. He's into guns.'

"What about handguns? Do you have one?"

Kovaks sensed more than saw the question's impact. Unconsciously now Fisher understood where they were headed. What did they know, he wondered? Who knew about the gun? Then the thunderbolt: Brenda.

"Um, yeah, I had one for a while. But I got rid of it."

"What make, caliber was it? Was it a revolver?"

"Oh, I don't remember, maybe it was a .38. It was a revolver."

'He knows all about the rifle but can't recall details about the pistol. He's figured out we may have the bullet. His gun can't be the same caliber as the murder weapon, or we'll be suspicious.'

"Where'd you get it?" Wheeler was leaning forward, eyes locked on Fisher's.

"Uh, I bought it from a guy in the parking lot at the packing plant. He said he needed money. It was an impulse; I didn't really need one."

"Where is it now?"

"Oh, gosh, I don't know. I didn't like the thing, so I got rid of it"

"How did you dispose of it?"

"I sold it to another guy, over at Toledo's Bar. That was about a week ago."

Both officers sat back and waited.

A few beats later, Wheeler said, "Mr. Fisher, Travis was shot once in the chest. Usually that sounds like murder. But maybe something happened before that. Maybe there was an argument and Travis was threatening. Could be the shooting was self-defense. If Travis went behind a guy's back to win over Brenda, he was asking for it."

"Man, I didn't do anything. I went right home after I dropped Brenda off."

"Yeah, you said that. Brenda lives east of Wildwood and you live the other direction. When you dropped her off, you would have gone right by Travis' house. Did you stop by?"

"I didn't go straight home exactly. I drove around some to clear my head. I went out by the reservoir before I went back."

"But you just said, 'I went right home.'"

"Hey, I'm still hungover and I haven't had enough sleep. Can't we do this tomorrow?"

"I think we're close to the end, Mr. Fisher. Did you have the gun with you at the party?"

"Uh, no. Like I said, I sold it."

"Were you still high on the meth?"

"I told you, I don't think I used any. I was really drunk."

"We are going to talk to David. Do you think he'll remember? The lab says there are good prints on the straw."

"I don't know the guy; he might say anything to put blame on me. Look, I wouldn't hurt Travis, he was my friend."

Looking at her partner Kovaks said, "Well, Detective Wheeler, Mr. Fisher has told us some things. He says he smoked dope at the house but can't remember snorting meth. It didn't bother him that his girlfriend was in the bedroom with her top off, and Travis working her body. Or, somehow, she left her bra behind and wouldn't put out for

129

him when he took her home. He owned a handgun until he sold it a week ago. Conveniently, both transactions happened in ways that can't be traced. Oh, he can't remember the make or caliber, even though he has the details of his hunting rifle. He says he was drunk and may have used some meth, but he went out for a drive after dropping off his girlfriend. This doesn't add up."

Fisher looked from one to the other, searching for an ally. His eyes had opened wider, pupils still dilated. He bowed his head and examined his hands.

Gently Wheeler said, "Mr. Fisher, if we arrest you, we're going to swab your hands. Unless you washed up with acetone, there's going to be gunshot residue that would be hard to explain. Is there anything you want to tell us?"

A long minute passed silently. Kovaks had one card left to play.

"Charlie, it looks like you haven't been in trouble before. You may not know how the system works. The DA decides what charges to bring. Cooperation counts. If you went back to Travis' house clear headed and killed him, then that's murder, 25 years to life. If, though, you were so upset about him laying hands on Brenda, and high on meth, then it might be a heat of passion crime. We can't promise anything, but manslaughter is 10 years, not 25. You could give yourself a future."

Fisher had gone quiet. Finally, he said, "I need time to think, OK?"

Watching from the mirrored window, they saw Fisher working his jaw, as though in conversation with himself. He shook his head as in disbelief and studied his hands. He imagined the invisible residue that would be his undoing. Looking at the mirror he called out, "All right."

They knocked and re-entered.

"Ok, Charlie, what's it going to be?" The use of his first name was intended to maintain connection.

His head down and visibly diminished, shoulders hunched, Fisher stared at the floor. "I couldn't believe that he was touching Brenda in front of me. It was like he was taunting me. When I went back there, I found the bra on the ground. I took another hit of meth. I had the gun in the car. The more I thought about it, the hotter I got. I didn't give him a chance to explain. I was tired of losing girls to guys like him. I backed him into the living room and shot him. That gunshot was so loud in there it shocked me. I watched him fall to the floor. It was like I came out of a coma, I knew I had to get out of there."

His commentary trailed off, losing focus.

"Do you still have the gun?"

"Yeah, it's in my dresser drawer. What happens now?"

"First, Mr. Fisher, you are under arrest for the murder of Travis Morgan."

"Wait, I thought you said manslaughter," Fisher protested desperately.

"Like I told you," Wheeler noted, "that's up to the DA. We'll tell them you helped us. You'll be appointed an attorney and he can bargain with the prosecution."

'You might want to tell us you're sorry about what happened to Travis', thought Wheeler as he placed handcuffs behind Fisher's back and led him out of the interrogation room.

Acknowledgments and Notes on the Stories

The Waiting Rooms.

My father was emotionally remote, so the relationship in this story is personal. Two close friends have died of cancer. The loss of dignity is horrible. Vern Katz, (MD ret.), gave me advice about terminology and the analgesic, *dilaudid*.

The So What.

My uncle, Eddie Wandro, owned the So What Tavern on the east side of Waterloo, Iowa. It was in proximity to the North End. De Facto segregation was as virulent as described. The minority population came from Holmes County, Mississippi to break the 1911 Illinois Central Railroad strike.

The Madam C.J. Walker method was a popular hair straightening process. The racial makeup of the police department was as depicted.

My thanks to Tim Kuhlmann of the Waterloo Public Library for newspaper archives about the first Black police officers. Herman Jackson and Ron Tinsley consulted their female relatives about hair straightening products and techniques. They also suggested the term "Negro" as that was the usage in 1959. Otherwise, the story is fictional.

Old Spot:

This is an elaboration of a tale I heard somewhere.

The Orion:

Cordova, Alaska's history and economic decline are historically described. In 1998, it sponsored its first cruise ship as a port-of-call. The passengers were 500 gay men, a fact unknown to town officials. That voyage was followed a week later by 500 lesbians. The last arrival that season was packed with "old farts" who caused the most trouble with complaints, bickering among themselves and shoplifting at the Museum.

There was a drive-through liquor store operated by Mimi Briggs, my model for Mary Kennedy. Al Cave gave me additional insight about Cordova. Brian Pemberton counseled me about Reverse Osmosis water systems. Dave Weil gave me specifications for the *Orion*.

The King cruise line, the *Orion,* the ship breakdown, and aftermath are fictional. The Iceworm Festival has been held every February since 1961.

An Agnostic's Journey:

This story was inspired by a cartoon depicting people in an airplane with the caption: 'I find the trip goes much faster if I have someone to convert.' A couple of fundamentalists shared their views with me.

The Phone Call:

Urologist Jeff Woolsey assisted with technical advice about transplants.

The Interrogation:

Retired Sheriff's Detective Kurt Wuest offered a critical review of police protocol, correcting several misimpressions.

About the Author

Jack Billings is a retired jurist and attorney. His writing career began in 2016 as he authored four magazine articles which were featured in both domestic and foreign on-line and print media.

They were derived from his international and United States river adventures and a flotilla cruise through the Inside Passage of British Columbia. In late 2019, he turned his attention to fiction and dialogue.

This collection of stories is his fictional debut. He and his wife, Linda DeSpain, live near Eugene, Oregon.

Made in the USA
Columbia, SC
17 June 2024